Abe Katz & Chana Leah

Dora Katz & Jacob Silverstein

MinnieKatz & Bernie Wolff

Simon Katz

Rosalyn Silverstein & George Blumberg

Sylvia Silverstein

Selma Wolff

Bennie Wolff

Alvin Wolff

Rose Wolff

Morris Wolff

Lee Ann Blumberg & David Marlowe

Lori Sue Blumberg

D1360168

The Fourth Corner

Libby Rosenblum Werthan

gefen
publishing house בית הוצאה לאור
JERUSALEM ◆ NEW YORK

Typesetting: Marzel A.S. – Jerusalem
Cover Design: Studio Paz, Jerusalem
Illustrations: Gill Fridman

1 3 5 7 9 8 6 4 2

Gefen Publishing House
POB 36004, Jerusalem 91360, Israel
972-2-538-0247 • orders@gefenpublishing.com

Gefen Books
12 New Street Hewlett, NY 11557, USA
516-295-2805 • gefenbooks@compuserve.com

www.israelbooks.com

Printed in Israel

Send for our free catalogue

ISBN 965-229-275-3

Library of Congress Cataloging-in-Publication Data:
Werthan, Libby Rosenblum, 1937-
The fourth corner / Libby Rosenblum Werthan.
1. Jews—Tennessee—Nashville—Fiction. 2. Nashville (Tenn.)—Fiction.
3. Jewish families—Fiction. I. Title.
PS3623.E77F68 2001 • 813'.6—dc21 • 2001033516

EPIGRAPH

Bring us in peacefulness from the four corners of
the earth and lead us with upright pride to our land.

Blessing of the Shema, a Hebrew prayer

Contents

PREFACE

This book of simple short stories is a gift first and foremost to our children and grandchildren — it is a part of their history, their legacy.

Secondly, it is a gift to our friends in Jerusalem, most of whom know little of the Southern Jews and have always shown a curiosity about this special life style.

And thirdly, but certainly not least, to the Jewish community of Nashville, Tennessee, which nurtured me and provided the soil and substance of these stories.

It is an attempt to capture in fiction the unique quality of life in a small and remote Jewish community in a particular time frame. It is, for the most part, my time frame and my community, but it is not an autobiography. I am not Lee Ann and Lee Ann is not I. But she lived on my turf and shared my experiences. Some of the incidents in the stories have their seeds in reality, most are pure fiction. If one believes them to be true or if one sees oneself in them, then I have succeeded in my quest.

One does not complete an endeavor of this sort without the help of others. My gratitude goes to my husband, Moshe, who read and reread each story, corrected my spelling and grammar, and made me believe that I could do it. I am grateful, too, to my mother, Baylie Rosenblum, whose insights guided me and whose knowledge of Nashville is boundless, and to Minnie

Berlin, who graciously gave of her time to fill me in on a period that was before my time.

The late Professor Howard Harrison, of Jerusalem, was of valuable assistance, as were the members of his writing seminar. Yechezkel Mink encouraged me to publish my work.

Libby Rosenblum Werthan

Jerusalem, 2001

JOURNEY

❦ 1951 ❧

Lee Ann sat on the footstool in front of Papa Ben's chair, unbuckling her book satchel. Papa Ben sat patiently watching Lee Ann take out the spiral notebook and yellow pencil.

"You know," he said, "this is the first time I've ever been interviewed."

Papa Ben's voice was deep and tinged with an accent he swore he didn't have.

"So," he continued, "tell me what this is all about."

"Well, you see, they have this contest all over the United States for ninth graders. To enter you have to write a paper on what citizenship means to you, and the one that writes the best paper gets to go to Washington and meet the president. Miss Alcott is making us all write essays. I really didn't know what to write, but Daddy said that I ought to talk to you because you weren't just born a citizen, you had to become one. So I thought maybe you could tell me about that."

Ben looked down at his granddaughter as she spoke. The pretty little girl was growing up. Her face, although still round and plump, was developing character. Her bright hazel eyes were almost hypnotic in their intensity. Her thick brown hair was pulled back into a ponytail that bounced as she explained her mission. His son had warned him she was coming and had told him what she wanted. He was ready for her, he hoped. This would be their first grownup conversation and he wanted it to go well.

It had made Ben think about things long forgotten, things that had happened almost fifty years ago. Somehow he never talked about those things. They had happened. His family had lived through them. But there was always something new going on, and what happened then didn't seem all that important. But he had saved the letters. And now here was his granddaughter asking him questions about them.

"Well, Papa Ben, I guess we should start with where you came from and why you came to America."

"That sounds good to me. Let's see, I was born in Mogilev, Russia, in 1887."

"That was another century."

"Yes, it was. When I was sixteen, in 1903, I left Russia and came to America."

"You came all alone? Why did you come?"

"In Russia, when a boy got to be sixteen, he was inducted into the Russian army, and my parents did not want that to happen to me."

Lee Ann put down her pencil. Her face grew solemn.

"Papa Ben, I don't think I can write about this."

"Why not, Lee Ann?"

"Because it sounds so…so…unpatriotic, and this is an essay on patriotism. I mean, leaving Russia to avoid military service. It doesn't seem right. I thought this family believed in fighting for your country. Daddy did."

"It's not what you're thinking, Lee Ann. Russia wasn't America. And the Russian army wasn't anything like the American army. They took young boys and many were never heard from again. It was cruel. Especially for a religious Jewish boy. You couldn't be Jewish in the army. And the length of service was twenty-five years. Even if you could survive, you wouldn't be the same person who went in. It was so bad that parents of friends of mine cut off their sons' fingers or toes, so that they would be unfit for the military.

Lee Ann, my parents couldn't do that. So they sent their oldest son off to family in America. I had to leave everyone I knew and head off to God knows what, with only some gold coins sewn in my jacket and a pack on my back. I had to walk, hitchhike, bribe border guards, go without food...things you can't imagine."

"Why didn't I know any of this?"

"I just never talked about it, not even to my sons. Once I got here, it didn't seem important. Maybe I was wrong."

Ben reached over and took a worn leather packet off the end table. He undid the string tied around it.

"I did save these. These are the letters I wrote to my family and the ones that I got back. I thought they might help you understand that time. I'll have to read them to you. They are written in Yiddish. I'll have to translate."

"Oh, let me see, Papa Ben!"

Papa Ben handed the letters to Lee Ann. She could tell they were very old. The paper was brittle, the ink faded, and the writing unfamiliar.

"Which ones were from you?"

Papa Ben pointed to the larger, bolder print.

"I wrote that and the others were from Little Bubbie, *aleha hashalom*."

"I would like to hear them."

"It might be slow going, I haven't read Yiddish in a long, long time."

Nov. 10, 1903
Indianapolis, Indiana

Dear Mamma and Tata,

Well, I am finally here. As you can see from the date, it took me a very long time and the trip was hard, but I didn't get robbed and I arrived here in one piece. Mama, I had to spend some of the gold coins you sewed into my jacket to bribe the border guards and for the train, but I have five left.

Cousin Stanley met me at the station. He is Uncle Samuel's (Shmuel) oldest son. He is twenty — almost four years older than I am. He drove to the station in the family's big black carriage with two horses. They are very rich. They live in a big house with electric lights and indoor toilets. Aunt Hannah is a very elegant lady.

They have made a room for me in the basement, but it is clean and warm. Uncle Samuel says that I will start to work in his factory on Monday. I will be going to school at night to learn English. Outside of the family no one speaks Russian, and not too many people I have met so far speak Yiddish.

Everything is a new experience and I am puzzled most of the time. I am sure that I will learn a lot very quickly.

I miss all of you very much and am homesick for Mama's cooking. How is the inn, Tata? Do you have time to study with Reb Yehuda?

Please tell Yitzchak and the girls I miss them.

Your son,
Benjamin

❖   ❖   ❖

"They didn't have cars then?"

"Not yet."

"In Russia, you were very poor?"

"We didn't think we were very poor. We were better off than a lot of others. But yes, I guess we were very poor."

"What was the inn?"

"Reb Daniel, my father, ran the inn. It was our place of business. My father was the head of the Jewish community, an important man."

❖ ❖ ❖

January 2, 1904
Mogilev, Russia

My dearest, darling son,

You don't know how much joy it gave us to get your letter. We have been so worried and dreamed a million dreams about all the terrible things that could have happened to you on your journey. But now you are safe in the arms of your family! Do not spend the gold coins. Keep them for an emergency. Please G-d, you will not have an emergency, but you never know.

We are all fine. It is very cold here now as you well know, but we have plenty of wood, thanks to G-d. Tata works hard. He takes terrible chances, but you know Tata. Usually he doesn't have any trouble with the Cossacks because he is so big and tall, but the other night there was a group of them singing and drinking at the inn, and one of them pushed Yitzchak as he was bringing them more vodka. Well, Tata saw him do it, and he ran over and picked the man up by his belt and collar and threw him out in the snow. Thank G-d everyone quieted down, but you never know.

Tata doesn't get as much time to learn as he would like (he is a great scholar, it's a shame!) but with the inn and everyone coming to him for advice and help, there is not much left. Do you have time to learn? Where is the Rabbi from?

The girls and Yitzchak are fine. Yitzchak is in love. Jacob's little sister, Sophie. Benjamin, we need to find a way to come there soon. Yitzchak turns sixteen next year and you know what that means.

They took Reuven, Golda's son, last week. A terrible thing!

Stay well and stay warm. We think about you every minute.

Much love from all of us,

Mama

❖ ❖ ❖

"Who were the Cossacks?"

"They were the cavalry. They could cause a lot of trouble for the Jews. Sometimes we had pogroms."

"Pogroms?"

"Large groups of Cossacks would come into the village and hurt and kill people."

"Couldn't you call the police?"

"They were the police."

"Weren't you afraid?"

"Tata wouldn't let us be afraid."

❖ ❖ ❖

April 12, 1904
Nashville, Tennessee

Dear Family,

I hope you can forgive me for what I am about to tell you. I wished so much that I could have talked to you about it, but there was no way, and the opportunity came up and I took it.

I am in Nashville, Tennessee, and this is how I got here. I know

Uncle Samuel is Tata's brother, but he is nothing like Tata. I did not like living there. I slept in the basement, which wasn't so terrible, but the family was ashamed of me and that was terrible. If they had company for supper, I had to eat in the kitchen by myself. They never took me with them anywhere, even to *shul*. I had to go alone. At the factory, the only work Uncle Samuel gave me was sweeping up and taking out the garbage. I was so humiliated.

Tata, please forgive me for being so proud. I know it is a sin, and I also do not want to cause trouble in the family. But what's done is done.

I made a friend in my English class, a boy like myself from Minsk. He told me that he heard of a factory in Nashville, Tennessee, that makes pants. It's owned by Jewish people and they were looking to hire Jewish workers. He told me he was going and asked me to come along. So I did.

At the factory, I am a cutter and I make enough to put a little aside each week. They have banks here where you can put your money and it will be safe. There is a Jewish settlement house here in Nashville where they helped us find a room with a Jewish family. A *hamish* Jewish family and the lady knows how to cook. There is a *shul* nearby and the Jewish people here are very friendly.

Tata, there is a problem with this, and I don't exactly know how to tell you in a letter. The factory where I work is open on *Shabbos*. There is no work here that is not open on *Shabbos*. It is their market day. They work six days a week in America and rest on Sundays. There are mostly *goyim* here. So I cannot go to shul on *Shabbos* morning, only on Friday night. Please try to understand. When you get here you will understand.

I will tell you about Nashville because it will be your home, I hope, soon. It is much farther south than Indianapolis and the weather is milder. When I first got here, the city was very sooty because it is surrounded by hills which keep the smoke from the coal furnaces in, so my first impression wasn't so good, but now it is spring, and the air is clear and the city is beautiful. It is very green here, with many trees and beautiful flowers and parks and a river. There is a kosher butcher and bakery and three *shuls* of different kinds. You will like it, I know.

I am sorry to be so happy when I know I may have caused you pain.

From now on you can write me in care of Goldstein — 23 Gay Street — Nashville, Tennessee.

Your Loving Son,
Ben

"I guess they didn't have telephones back then. You had to wait so long to get a letter. Weren't you homesick?"

"Terribly, but I couldn't let them know that."

May 18, 1904
Mogilev, Russia

Dear Benjamin,

Tata and I agree. You did the right thing! Tata was very, very angry with Shmuel, but he has calmed down some. It's a good thing there are so many miles between them.

It sounds like, thank G-d, our prayers were answered and you have made a good move, although Tata is worried about your *Yiddishkeit*. I told him that you are in a Jewish home and you will do the best you can. Please thank the Goldsteins for us, and we look forward to meeting them.

Yitzchak and the girls have an English book that they are

studying, but we are having a problem with Yitzchak. He says he cannot and will not go to America. He will not leave Sophie. Can you believe this? After all we are going through for him. If it were you, I could understand, but Yitzchak? What does that little *pitsele* know about love? I keep thinking it will pass, but now I am not sure. What to do? Tata says keep out of it, but that's not possible. We will be leaving in six months!

I am enclosing a list of questions from the girls. They want to know everything about Nashville and what life is like there. Tata doesn't ask too many questions and that worries me. I know he thinks about what will be, and I suspect that he is concerned whether there will be a place for him there. He is a very important man here. What will he be there?

If it wouldn't cost too much, could you maybe send us a picture of you?

Your loving,
Mama

❖ ❖ ❖

"Yitzchak is Uncle Izzy?"
Ben nodded.

❖ ❖ ❖

July 4, 1904
Nashville, Tennessee

Dear Tata, Mama, Yitzchak, Fannie and Jennie,

You will never believe what is happening here today. It is the Fourth of July and the celebration of American Independence and everyone is going crazy. They had a big parade down the main street of town

with bands and clowns and decorated carriages with flowers, and
even horseless carriages — automobiles. Have you seen one? Last
month they had an automobile race here. It was something to see.
The horseless carriage is the wave of the future. Every American boy
dreams of riding in one.

By next July, I will be a citizen. I am in the citizenship class and
am learning all about the American government and democracy.
Then I will really be able to celebrate. Did you know that Nashville is
the capital of the State of Tennessee? The State Capitol building is
very grand. It sits on a big hill in the middle of the city, and it is only
a block from where I live. I can see it from the front room window.

Fannie and Jennie — I never saw so many questions. *Gevalt!* I
don't know the answers to many of them, but I have a friend, a very
nice girl that I met at a *shul* social. She was born here. Can you
believe that? And she knows everything about Nashville. So I am
asking her to write to you.

The Tennessee State Capitol Building

I can tell you a few things. Yes, there are unmarried Jewish boys here. It is a strange thing, but there are two sets of Jews here. The first set is like us. Their prayers are like ours; they speak Yiddish and come from Russia, Poland and Hungary. Most have been here only a few years. They work in the big factories or have small shops. The second group has been here many years. They came from Germany mainly, and they already have stores and businesses and live outside downtown. They remind me of Aunt Hannah in that they are elegant, but in general they are more pleasant. They are helpful, too. They are the ones that run the settlement house and helped me find a place to live. But they go to a different shul and have different customs and are separated from us in that way.

Yes, English is a difficult language, but the people here speak slowly, so you will be able to catch on. I am doing very well with my English and it's been less than a year.

Yes, they do have amazing stores here (some of them owned by Jews). You can buy dresses all ready made — more dresses than you have ever seen. No, there is no ice-skating here and not much snow, and today it is very, very hot, with moisture in the air that makes it very heavy. They have big factories that only make ice. They use the ice to cool their food, and they also put small pieces of it into their water to drink to cool themselves down. The women dress in lightweight cotton dresses and some of them do not wear stockings.

They have a food they call ice cream that is very popular here and very delicious. It comes in different flavors — chocolate, vanilla, and strawberry. You will love it! They also have a fruit here that you have never seen. It is called watermelon and is very large and green on the outside, but on the inside it is quite red and juicy. They put it in the ice to get it very cold, and then it is very refreshing.

They don't have ice-skating but they do have something called roller-skating (instead of a blade there are four little wheels on the bottom), and there is a rink in a wonderful park called Glendale. You get there by taking an electric streetcar! There is a merry-go-round there and even a roller coaster. I will take you. I am putting in a picture that was taken at Glendale Park. The pretty girl with me in the picture is Pearl. She's the girl who is going to write to you.

There are many beautiful homes to be seen when you ride the streetcar and a very grand university called Vanderbilt, with many large and interesting buildings. They are even building a skyscraper downtown that will have twelve stories! Also there is another park here that has a replica of the Parthenon of Greece. It is so big. It was a kind of heathen temple, but it is only used for show now. I wasn't sure that a Jewish boy should go in it, but everyone does.

Two other things that they have here that you have never seen are baseball and *shvartzes*. Baseball is a game that is played with a ball and a stick and is very popular. *Shvartzes* are people with very black skin but in all other ways seem to be like other people. They used to be slaves, like we were in Egypt, but here in America — can you believe that? In some ways they are still doing the work of slaves but they get paid for it.

There are too many things here to tell you about in one letter. Pearl will write you, too. But remember that everything here is not all good, there are poor people here, too. But we are young and strong and smart, and those that have these qualities seem to do well here.

Mama, Mrs. Goldstein has her eyes open for a house for us, and I know a place where we can get furniture cheap.

Tata, I am told that people here can keep a few cows in their backyards and walk them down to a meadow called Sulpher Dell to graze them. Maybe that will be a possibility for us. Also I found a very learned young man named Fishman, who is looking for a *chevrusah* and I told him about you. He is very eager for you to come.

I love you all.

Ben

❖   ❖   ❖

"You met Grandma Pearl when you were sixteen?"

"Seventeen."

"How old were you when you got married?"

"Nineteen."

"That was young."

"We grew up quick back then."

Sept. 1, 1904
Mogilev, Russia

My darling son,

We are fast approaching the holidays and everyone is making preparations, but I cannot keep from letting thoughts of our upcoming journey get in the way. Thank G-d, all the arrangements seem to be going smoothly and we will have enough money to do it. We received the money you sent and that will be a help. Thank you so much and G-d bless you.

The authorities have agreed to let us have the necessary papers, but listen to this. You know the problem we have been having with Yitzchak on account of Sophie. Well, Yitzchak, in his *chutzpedihk* way, has come up with a plan.

Why not take Sophie with us, he says. The authorities still have us listed as having two sons and two daughters. So he says we could dress Sophie up like a boy (G-d forgive us) and bring her with us as the other son. Would you believe he has talked her mama and papa into this *meshugaas*! So you better tell Mrs. Goldstein that we may need an extra bedroom.

Thank you for finding a *chevrusah* for Tata. He is looking forward. As hard as the life is here, it is also hard to leave. It is all we have ever known. I wish that we had *mishpacha* there, but I guess we will never speak to Uncle Shmuel again and we will have to make our own family. Speaking of this, what about the *sheine meidl* in the picture? Is this the girl for you? What is her *yiches*? Who are her people?

We will send you all the information about our journey very soon. We love you.

Shana tova,
Mama

❖   ❖   ❖

"What's a hev…"

"*Chevrusah*? It's someone you learn with. A partner."

"What were they learning?"

"Torah and Talmud."

"Why? Why did they do that?"

"Do what?"

"Study about Torah and Talmud."

"Just because. Just because that was what you were supposed to do in those days."

"What was *yiches*?"

"*Yiches* was, um, kind of family. She wanted to know if Grandma Pearl came from the right kind of family."

"Did she?"

"No, she was Hungarian. But they liked her anyway, so it all worked out."

"Was that the last letter?"

"It was."

"And so they came and everything worked out."

Papa Ben nodded. "More or less. Do you think you have enough material for your essay?"

Lee Ann smiled. "Papa Ben, I think I'm on my way to Washington."

"Just a minute," said Papa Ben as he reached in his pocket. "Give me your hand, you might need this for the journey."

Lee Ann looked down at the gold coin and closed her fingers around it.

ROSALYN

❦ 1929 ❦

Rosalyn glanced up at the blackening sky. Heavy clouds were moving in, and the electricity prickled her bare arm even before the first bolt of lightning lit up the sky. She counted...one and, two and, three and, four and...BOOM. Four miles away and coming fast, she thought, as she began running up Union Street. Fat drops of rain and the pelt of tiny hailstones caught her just as she reached the steps of the YMHA building. I hate thunder. I hate lightning. I hate storms. Please God, I want to live someplace without storms.

She paused under the canopy at the top of the steps to catch her breath. Through the glass-paned doors she could see the yellowish light reflected warmly on the cracked brown leather couches and the dark tile floor of the lobby. She knew this building by heart. Just to the left of the lobby was a small multi-purpose room where the girl scouts held their awards ceremony each year, and behind that was the males-only poolroom, the domain of Mr. Irv with his shiny bald head and his quiet awareness. At the very back of the lobby was the gymnasium with its weights and horses, its parallel bars and floor mats, its nets and baskets, and the sweet-sour odor of sweat. This, too, was essentially a male place, except when the girls played volleyball or the dance club worked on its new routines. Below the gym, in the basement, was an indoor pool, which, even though it had been years ago that Solly Greenberg had pushed her under, still made her squeamish.

Rosalyn brushed the rain off her face and went inside. As she passed the office on her right, she waved to the receptionist and checked the wall clock. Twenty minutes to spare before her scout meeting. She raced upstairs to the second floor and into the scout room. It was empty. Even Miss Ida, the troop leader, hadn't arrived. She quickly put her book satchel on a chair, adjusted the yellow tie of her uniform and left the room.

At the end of the hall, she opened a door silently and entered the balcony section of the gym. He was there. She knew he would be.

The Young Men's Hebrew Association Building (YMHA) — 1924-1948

He came every day right after school. She heard him even before she saw him — the soft grunts of exertion — the slap of his hands on the horse. Peering over the railing, she saw him in the far corner, the white of his pants and shirt gleaming in the otherwise dreary room. Outside, she could hear the storm raging, but in the gym she felt safe. She watched, captivated by the grace in his movements, the perfection of his body, his solitary pursuit. She loved him. She knew it must be love, because a feeling like a wash of warm liquid came over her every time she saw him.

The hands on the clock over the basketball goal stood at 3:30 and she knew she must go. It was satisfying to Rosalyn that her secret visit hadn't disturbed his rhythm, that the soft grunts would go on even without her.

❖ ❖ ❖

She didn't know why she had let it slip out to her mother. She hadn't even told her best friend, Becky, and she usually told her everything. Mama was so mean about it, so heartless.

"Forget it, Rosalyn, he's not for you."

"But you don't even know him, Mama."

"Just take my word for it."

"But why not, Mama?"

"Just keep your distance."

That had ended the conversation and Rosalyn hadn't pushed it. It wasn't a good idea to rile up Mama. But she felt her stomach knotting and knew that she had allowed the privacy of her feelings to be invaded, the purity of her emotions tainted. Her mother had not put the stamp of approval on her choice, and it dulled but did not stop what she felt.

Later that same night, she overheard her mother retelling the conversation to her father. She couldn't hear the words, but the tone indicated that he agreed. Hot tears welled up and she cried softly into her pillow. In all her fifteen years, she had never defied her parents, but she was so drawn to Samuel Marlowe that she could no longer trust herself.

Spring lengthened into summer, and the afternoon storms continued to roll in from the West, sometimes wreaking havoc in their wake — an upturned tree, a fallen branch, power outages. When the school year ended, Rosalyn went to work in her father's office. She was there every day from 8:00 until 3:00, leaving her late afternoons and evenings free. Since she was already downtown, she signed up for late afternoon classes at the YMHA on Tuesdays and Wednesdays, helped her mother on Mondays with the laundry and on Thursdays with the cooking for Shabbat. Saturdays and Sundays were hers. She rarely attended Shabbat services, preferring to lie in bed on Saturday mornings until 11:00 or later, then spend the day reading a good book. On Sunday afternoons the family — her mother, father and younger sister, Sylvia — would pack up a picnic supper of fried chicken, potato salad, dill pickles, home-grown tomatoes, a big jug of iced tea and rugalah for dessert. They would pile in the car and head for Centennial Park. Sunday afternoons in the park were a ritual only interrupted occasionally by the summer storms, which didn't deter them from going but often sent them scurrying for cover under the band shelter.

Most of the Jewish families Rosalyn knew were usually at the park, too. It was the hub of their social life. The men talked about business and the condition of the world, and especially the condition of the Jews in that world; the women talked about children, style, food, and prices; the younger kids played games or went to the small lake and fed the ducks bits of bread. Some of the bigger boys liked to fish and would bring bags of soft dough to use for bait on the hooks of the cane poles they rented at the concession stand. The teenagers and young singles would move off in small groups, sometimes talking, sometimes singing, but always flirting.

Later, after the trash was thrown away, the baskets repacked,

The Vine Street Jewish Temple — Reform — 1876-1950

and the sky had turned inky black, they went home. Some of the kids would end up at Rosalyn's house. They'd roll up the rug in the front room, start the player piano, and dance until midnight. There were always plenty of pretzels and popcorn in the pantry and apple cider in the icebox. Rosalyn was always amazed that her mother never objected. It was one of the few things that her mother tolerated.

Samuel Marlowe and his friends, the Temple crowd, never came to the park. Where did they go on Sunday afternoons, Rosalyn wondered. The Woodmont Country Club, she guessed. She had never been there, and the enormous hedge that separated it from the road revealed nothing. But she knew it must be a wondrous place with tennis courts, a golf course, a swimming pool, and people dressed in lounging outfits, like the ones she'd seen in the pictures of cruise ships.

In a way she was glad that he wasn't at the park on Sundays. Tuesdays were bad enough. She hadn't realized when she signed up for the art class at the Y that Samuel would be there, too. But he was. Twelve easels had been set up in the reception hall. The instructor liked the way the late afternoon sun came in the high windows, casting long shadows across the still lifes. The class was a mixture of young and old — seven girls, two women, a man and two boys. Mr. Roth, the instructor, had put Rosalyn's easel next to Samuel's.

"Hi, I'm Samuel Marlowe. What's your name?"

"Rosalyn...Rosalyn Silverstein."

"Why haven't I seen you before?"

"I don't know, I'm around here all the time."

"Do you go to the Temple?"

"No."

The class started. They would be working on pencil sketches first — a bowl of fruit. At the break, she sneaked a peek at Samuel's work. She marveled at the detail, the texturing. Beside it, her work looked flat and drab. She shifted her easel away from his view. When they came back after the break, she could sense Samuel looking her way, but he wasn't looking at her work, he was looking at her. She felt the blood rise to her cheeks. What did he see? She knew she was pretty. Everyone told her. Her brown-black hair was thick and wavy, and she tied it back with a wide red satin ribbon. Her skin was pale and clear with a pinkish glow, her lips full, her nose straight. It was her eyes that attracted the attention. Heavy lashes over oval-shaped green eyes set in such a way that they seem to be looking into one's very soul.

They hardly spoke again until the third week.

"Where do you live?" He had asked.

"Central Avenue."

"Would you like a ride home?"

"No, thank you. Papa's office is just down the street. I ride home with him."

"The Fourth of July celebration at the Club is Sunday night. You know, fireworks and watermelon. Would you like to go with me?"

Rosalyn could feel her heartbeat quicken. "We're...I'm not a member."

"That's okay. We can bring guests."

"I don't know. I'll have to ask my parents."

"It's just a Fourth of July celebration. It won't be late. I can drive. I have a license, but if they would rather, my father could drive us. How old are you, anyway?"

"I'll be sixteen in the Fall. How old are you?"

"Eighteen last month."

Her parents did not take the news lightly.

Her mother — "I told you before, it's not something you should get mixed up with. There are plenty of nice Jewish boys at the synagogue, boys your own age, boys with parents we know."

Her father — "Honey, I don't want to see you get into a situation where you are bound to get hurt."

Rosalyn — "Just tell me what's wrong with it. Is there a law against a synagogue person going with a temple person? They are Jews, aren't they? What makes you so sure I'll get hurt? He is very nice and polite. Kind of shy in a way. It's not like I don't know anything. I'm almost sixteen and I can take care of myself."

Her mother — "Go! But don't come whining back to us. Those people will never accept you."

She had agonized all week over what to wear, finally settling on a white sleeveless linen sheath trimmed in royal blue and her new white sandals. Instead of the red ribbon she usually wore, she tied a red silk scarf of her mother's around her ponytail.

Samuel came for her in a black sedan. Her mother accompanied her to the door. Samuel, smiling broadly and showing a perfect set of white teeth said: "I am very glad to meet you, Mrs. Silverstein. So nice of you to let Rosalyn join me this evening. I will drive her over. I am a very careful driver and my father will drive us back later. We won't be late. He likes to get to bed at a decent hour."

Mama couldn't help but be impressed by that, Rosalyn thought. He's such a perfect gentleman — and his teeth! How many times has Mama said that her criteria for good looks were a perfect set of teeth? But her mother's face conveyed little. A mask, Rosalyn thought, she's wearing her mask. Rosalyn had seen that look before, and it was impossible to know what lay behind it. Was it disapproval or just that her thoughts were a million miles away? Was it a sick headache coming on or something worse? I won't let it spoil my good time. Papa can handle it this time.

Once in the car, Rosalyn unintentionally let out a little sigh.

"Are you all right?"

"I'm fine. Do your parents worry about you a lot?"

"I guess so. Not so much the everyday stuff, but the big things like going to the best college and meeting the right friends and bringing honor to the family name. Stuff like that. They worry that I am too much a loner. They want me to play team sports, not spend my time on gymnastics. But they really don't bother me too much about it. And you?"

"Me?"

"Do your parents worry about you a lot?"

"Umm, well, they think I'm hard-headed. At least Mama does. She says I have a mind of my own — but who would want to have someone else's mind?"

Samuel chuckled.

"You might have noticed that she wasn't overjoyed for me to go with you tonight."

"Worried about the driving?"

Rosalyn shook her head.

"I'm too old for you?"

"No."

"What then?"

"You really don't know?"

Samuel glanced over at her. He looked puzzled. "Is this some kind of game?"

"I'm sorry! No. It's just that my parents...I guess most of the people I know think that you should go out with your own kind, that people from the synagogue shouldn't date people from the temple. It's like breaking an unwritten law. You can't tell me you don't know that. What did your parents say when you told them about me?"

"Nothing. I didn't say whom I was bringing. They've got so much going on they hardly notice."

As they drove down the long winding road that led up to the rambling white frame clubhouse, the last rays of the sun were golden ribbons streaming across the manicured green expanse of the golf course. Rosalyn loved the utter quiet, the soft serenity. It was a sharp contrast to her increasing anxiety. She wished he had told his parents. She didn't relish being a surprise. She wondered who would be there that she knew. To whom would she talk? What would she say?

Samuel parked the car and came around to open the door for her. She saw at once that her dress had been a mistake. Bright colored beach towels had been laid out along the slope below the tennis courts. Couples and families were already making their choices and settling down. The women and girls wore sundresses with full skirts that spread out around them. Why had she worn the sheath? Stupid!

Samuel selected a towel for them and eased her down. "I'll be back in a minute, just go get us some drinks. What would you like?"

"Oh, lemonade, if they have it."

Her legs stuck out like two white sticks. No time for sunning. She tried tucking them underneath her. The sheath pulled uncomfortably tight around her. I'm going to be a wrinkled mess, she thought.

Samuel returned with their drinks — a lemonade for her and a tall glass of frothy beer for himself.

"Is that good?"

"What? The beer?"

"Yeah."

"I like it. You want a taste?"

Rosalyn took a sip, wrinkling up her nose and squeezing her eyes shut as the cool liquid slid down her throat.

"Really liked it, huh?" said Samuel.

"It tastes like pee pee."

"Oh? And you've tasted pee pee?"

"No!"

"Then how do you know that beer tastes like it?"

"There are some things that a person just knows."

Rosalyn was suddenly aware of a couple walking toward them, a tall stocky man with thick hair graying at the temples, and an equally tall stately blond woman.

"Good evening, son. Happy Fourth! And who is this lovely young lady?"said the man.

"Dad, Mother, this is Rosalyn Silverstein."

"Happy to meet you, my dear. Would you be one of the Louisville Silversteins?" said Mrs. Marlowe.

Rosalyn glanced at Samuel, puzzled by the question. Samuel quickly interjected, "No, she's one of the Nashville Silversteins."

"Oh, I don't think I know the family."

Mr. Marlowe smiled. "I bet you're Jakie Silverstein's daughter."

Rosalyn nodded.

"Who's that?" asked Reba Marlowe.

"Jakie Silverstein is the greatest pool player the YMHA ever had. I could never beat him, not once."

"You played pool at the YMHA?"

"In my youth. Everyone wanted to play Jakie. So tell me, Rosalyn, what is he doing now?"

"He rents apartments."

"Oh, real estate."

The conversation was interrupted by the blare of a megaphone announcing the beginning of the fireworks display.

"We'd best find our seats. We'll see you at the clubhouse afterwards," said Phillip Marlowe.

BOOM! The sky lit up in a blaze of color — gold, red and purple. Then another and another. For fifteen minutes, Rosalyn was transported into a wonderland of bright sprays, rockets, and golden droplets. At the end, a blazing red, white and blue flag and a trumpeter who led the standing crowd in the *Star Spangled Banner* and *God Bless America*.

Rosalyn was exhilarated. She felt so proud to be young and strong and American, and when Samuel took her hand, she was flush with excitement. To be here, with him, it was like a dream, like a story in one of her books.

As they walked slowly up to the clubhouse, clouds of smoke lingered in the still air.

"I'd like to stop at the ladies room, if I could."

"Sure, just meet me out by the pool when you are done."

One glance in the mirror of the ladies lounge proved her right about the dress. It was a wrinkled mess, and there was a grass stain on the hem. Rosalyn was trying to wipe it off with a dampened tissue, when the door to the lounge opened and the room was suddenly filled with a flurry of chatter and giggles. Rosalyn looked up and recognized one of the three girls coming in. It was Dorothy Gold, who was in her dance club at the Y.

"Oh, Rosalyn, it is *you*. I thought I saw you out on the lawn...and with Samuel Marlowe. How did *you* ever do that?"

"Hi, Dorothy. Just lucky, I guess."

"Well, you are certainly looking very patriotic tonight...if slightly wilted."

Rosalyn bit her lip and turned back toward the mirror.

"Come on, girls. We'd better hurry. Can't keep the boys waiting. See you, Rosalyn."

Out by the pool hot dogs were sizzling on grills, and candlelit tables were laid out with potato salad, cole slaw, deviled eggs, and watermelon. She found Samuel, and he handed her a plate with a hot dog on a bun.

"I hope you like mustard and relish," he said. "Let's go over to the table, so you can pick out what else you want."

When they had filled their plates, they found a spot on the stone retaining wall and sat down to eat. Reba Marlowe, who had her arm around an attractive girl with brilliant red hair, quickly joined them.

"Samuel, I want you to meet Florence Adler. She's the daughter of Alfred Adler, Daddy's friend from St. Louis, and she's going to Radcliffe in the fall. The two of you will be on the same campus!"

While Samuel and Florence compared notes about their upcoming entrance into the university world in Cambridge, Reba turned her attention to Rosalyn.

"And where will you be matriculating, my dear?"

"Matric...?"

"Where will you be going to college?"

"Oh, I'm only a Junior."

"But surely you have given it consideration."

"Actually, no. If I go anywhere, it will probably be to secretarial school. Papa thinks I should have bookkeeping skills."

"Oh, I see," said Reba, and then, looking down at Rosalyn's plate, she added, "I'm surprised, I thought a nice Jewish girl like you would only eat kosher."

Rosalyn felt her stomach lurch. Kosher! This stuff she was eating was treif? At a Jewish club with all Jewish people! They were all eating *treif*!

"Are you all right, my dear?"

"Excuse me, I don't...I'm sorry, Mrs. Marlowe...excuse me," said Rosalyn as she turned and began running back to the clubhouse.

She almost collided with a white-jacketed waiter as she burst into the lobby. "Is there a phone here?" she asked.

"Yes'm, down the hall there."

She picked up the receiver and dialed her home. "Papa, it's Rosalyn, can you come and get me? Come now!"

❖ ❖ ❖

She waited inside the front doorway. Heat lightning became real lightning and sprinkles of rain began a soft patter on the roof. She could hear the members hurrying in from the pool area. Someone touched her arm.

"Rosalyn, I have been looking all over for you!"

She turned to face Samuel Marlowe. "I'm sorry, Samuel, I'm not feeling so well. Papa is coming for me."

"You didn't have to do that. I would have driven you."

"I didn't want to spoil your good time."

She heard the horn, and with a "thanks for everything," she ran out into the rain.

They drove slowly home, the windshield wipers laboring to clear away the battering rain.

"I hate storms, Papa. I wished we lived some place else, someplace where they don't have storms."

"Where would you want to live?"

"I don't know. Someplace. Maybe St. Louis or Louisville." Then she started to giggle. The giggle grew into laughter.

Jake Silverstein looked over at his wrinkled, tearful, hysterical daughter. "What's so funny?"

"Then we could be..." Rosalyn gulped for breath amid her laughter. "Then we could be the Louisville Silversteins."

WARTIME
❦ 1944 ❧

They are going to catch him. This time they are going to catch him and drag him out of the house...in handcuffs. Lee Ann pressed her nose against the dining room window. Her eyes searched the moonless night for the man on patrol, the air raid warden with his white armband and flashlight. The street was empty, only the slivers of light coming from the basement of the big white frame house across the street broke through the darkness.

Lee Ann was drawn to that house with its high ceilings, wood floors and...that forbidden basement. The chickens and dogs in the fenced in back yard made her think of a farm. But the Burtons weren't farmers. They lived in West Nashville in a neighborhood of simple houses, inhabited by God-fearing men and women of rural tastes and narrow perspectives.

She thought about that house a lot, almost as much as she thought about the ditch that cut a deep swath through her backyard next to the victory garden. In the winter the ditch was filled with rushing water that sometimes spilled over its banks and flooded the backyard. In the summer it was dry as a bone, the repository of countless treasures washed there by the deluge.

On that particular night in the summer of 1944, as she looked through the window, searching for the air raid warden, her imagination took over. She could see him walking slowly down Nevada, then turning onto her street. She could hear him gasp as he spotted the light peeking out from around the blankets Mr. Burton had tacked up over his basement windows. She could see him pull out a whistle and let out a blast so loud that air raid wardens from as far away as Alabama and Wyoming streets would come running. They would gather to stand and point to the windows, then rush to the basement door and, with all their might, break it down and drag Mr. Burton out onto the street. Of course, she would be the only one to see it, to tell the tale.

But just then the all-clear siren sounded and lights flashed on up and down the street.

"Lee Ann, honey, you better get yourself to bed. It's almost ten o'clock," Rosalyn Blumberg called out from the living room. "I bet there's not another six-year-old still awake in the whole city."

She climbed down from the chair, pushed it under the dining room table and went down the hall to her bedroom. Lori Sue was asleep in the other bed. She could hear Mama and Aunt Sylvia listening to Richard Harkness on the radio. Every night, they would sit on the floor in front of the big radio, take out the world map and try to find the places he talked about. But Mama was listening mainly for Iwo Jima because that's where Daddy was.

She turned off the lamp still thinking about Mr. Burton's basement. Even Katy, Mr. Burton's daughter, wasn't allowed in that basement. But once, the two of them had knelt down beside the window with their faces up close to the glass.

They cupped their hands around their heads to keep out the light and looked inside. In the shadows across the back wall were glass-covered bookcases. Some were filled with arrowheads and tomahawks mounted on white cardboard and others with feathery Indian head-dressings and stacks of Indian money beads. Spread out on the big table in the center of the room were more arrowheads and a scattering of books.

Then Katy shrieked, "Look!"

"Where?" Lee Ann responded, almost afraid to look.

"Over there on the floor! Right there next to the table! Look! Don't you see?"

There they were! Lying in a large metal box. Bones, real live human bones.

"Run!" Lee Ann screamed.

They headed for the hollowed out sticker bush in the front yard and crawled underneath. They sat there, two skinned-kneed little girls in shorts and tee shirts, one with short blond-white hair, the other with long flyaway brown, in their secret hiding place, catching their breath.

"I told you," whispered Katy.

They crossed their hearts and swore they would never tell. In a way, Lee Ann was sorry they had looked. It was one more thing she could never tell and she felt sneaky...not as sneaky as she had felt the time she was at Grandma Dora's and had spied on Tommy Adams next door taking a shower in the makeshift shower his father had rigged up in their garage. But sneaky enough.

Then Mama came in. "You still awake, Lee Ann?"

"Yeah, I was just thinking."

Mama pushed the hair out of her eyes. "About what?"

"About how Mr. Burton didn't get caught again."

"Oh, well, maybe next time," she said as she closed the door.

But Mr. Burton's going to dig up graves on the weekends wasn't the only odd thing about him. He didn't sleep in the big four-poster bed with Mrs. Burton. He slept on the day bed. Lee Ann knew because he stuck his chewing gum on the bedpost at night, and it was there when she came over to play. Of course, Daddy didn't sleep in the bed with Mama any more, being that he was overseas fighting in the War. Aunt Sylvia slept there now.

Mrs. Burton was kind of funny, too. They had a victory garden in their backyard. Everybody did. But they had chickens. Those chickens wandered all over the back yard cackling and carrying on and making their little chicken poop. Sometimes Mrs. Burton would chase a chicken and catch it. Katy and Lee Ann would high tail it for the kitchen and stand behind the screen door watching.

Mrs. Burton would take that chicken by the neck and swing it around and around until its head came off in her hand. She'd just stand there holding that chicken's head in her hand, the blood dripping down her arm, and that chicken would run all around the yard with no head, sloshing blood all over the grass and the pansies; the Thompson's dog, Buster, would let out a howl that you could hear all the way down to Charlotte Pike. It wasn't until Mrs. Burton had hung that chicken up by its feet from the clothesline that Kathy and Lee Ann would come out from behind the screen door.

Of course, Mr. and Mrs. Burton thought Lee Ann was odd, too. She knew, because sometimes they would look at each other out of the sides of their eyes and get real quiet. They ate stuff like white beans and ham hocks and thought it was good. Lee Ann didn't eat that stuff at her house because it wasn't kosher and they were Jewish, but sometimes, when she was at the Burton's, they would give her a taste of greens or grits with red eye gravy.

Mr. Burton would call her to the table and say, "Come here a minute, Lee Ann, and taste some one hundred percent American food."

Once, when she told them about the bag of fresh bagels Mr. Levy, the shirt salesman, had brought them from New York, they wanted to know what was a bagel. She said it was kind of the shape of a doughnut but it was hard.

"I never heard of such," said Mrs. Burton.

"Must be some kind of Jew food," said Mr. Burton, and then she saw them look at each other out of the sides of their eyes.

She couldn't believe they had never heard of a bagel, but then she found out that they had never heard of *gefilte fish* or chopped liver or *kishke*, so she figured that was Jew food, too.

Another thing that set their teeth on edge was that Lori Sue and Lee Ann had a colored woman come to their house every day to look after them. Nobody in West Nashville had colored women come to their houses.

When they lived in Cherokee Park with Papa Ben and Grandma Pearl, colored women came on the bus every day to clean peoples' houses and take care of their children. But in West Nashville, you never did see a colored person. That is, until Daddy went to the war. Then Mama had to run the store and she got Ada Baugh to come look after them.

Lee Ann remembered the first time she saw Ada. Mama had piled Lori Sue and her in the back seat of the car, and they had driven over to South Nashville. They had lots of colored people in South Nashville.

They pulled up to this little bitty house, and Mama went inside to get Ada. The house didn't have any paint on it and one side kind of drooped a little, but on the front porch in a rocking chair sat an old, old woman. Her skin was rust colored and all wrinkled, but her hair was the whitest white. Lee Ann was looking at her so hard that she almost didn't see Mama come out of the house with a tall colored woman in a red dress and white straw hat, carrying a bundle.

Mama opened the car door and said, "Scoot over girls, this is Ada Baugh."

Ada sat down beside them and put Lori Sue on her lap. "That's right," she said, "Ada from Decatur."

Driving home, they listened as she told Mama about how she grew up in Alabama and when her mama and daddy died had moved to Nashville.

"Who was that lady?" Lee Ann asked, looking at Ada.

"What lady," said Mama.

"The one in the rocking chair."

"Oh, that's my landlady," said Ada.

She may have been Ada's landlady, but from that moment on she was 'grandlady' to Lee Ann.

Ada became part of the family. She was there in the morning when Lori Sue and Lee Ann got up and was still there when they went to bed. The day Katy and Lee Ann found out that bees sting when you catch them by their wings and put them in a jar, it was Ada who pulled the stinger out with a tweezers, spit on some tobacco from one of Mama's cigarettes, and mashed it all over the hurt to take out the poison. It was Ada, too, who told Lee Ann that if she would tie a string around the wart on her thumb, then run around the house three times and bury the string in a secret place, her wart would fall off in just a week. Did too. Of course it was Ada who put Lee Ann over her knee on the back steps for God and everyone to see and gave her a big whack on her bottom when she ran across the street to Katy's without looking both ways.

The girls hardly ever saw Mama anymore because she was working so hard. And they only saw Aunt Sylvia at suppertime because she worked downtown at Castner Knott Department Store. Actually the only time they saw Mama was on Sundays and at noontime, when she would slip home to check the mailbox and grab a bite of lunch. She'd go through the mail searching for one of those army envelopes with Daddy's handwriting on it. Sometimes Daddy's letters would have big holes in them.

"The damn censors," Mama would say, "There's no privacy at all."

Sometimes there would even be a letter for Lee Ann. Daddy would draw pictures and print in words from the first grade reader so she could read them herself. She kept them in a red box under her bed. Once she got a package from Daddy. He sent her a bracelet he had made himself. It was made of silver metal and had a little Star of David cut out of the middle. He said it had come off of an airplane. Lee Ann loved it, but one day she buried it in Mama's talcum powder box so it would smell good and forgot where she put it for the longest time.

It seemed like all the daddies were in the army and all the mommies were working. Daddy didn't go at first. Only cousins and uncles went, people who didn't have wives or children. So they were hoping and praying that maybe the war would be over and Daddy wouldn't have to go. But then they ran out of cousins and uncles and had to take daddies and that was that.

Then they heard that the daddy of Janie Marie Phillips, who lived on the other side of the ditch, got wounded and he came home, only now one of his legs was made of wood and he could take it off. And Lee Ann heard, when she was at Grandma Dora's, that Tommy Adams' daddy was outright killed. She tried not to think of Daddy over there with all those Japs and bombs, but sometimes she had bad dreams about it and Aunt Sylvia would come and sleep with her.

Of course Lee Ann knew there was a lot of stuff going on that wasn't fit for children's ears. On Friday nights, Aunt Sylvia would take the girls over to Grandma Dora and Papa Jake's for *Shabbos* dinner. The table seemed kind of empty with all the uncles, cousins and daddies gone, just Papa Jake and Cousin Harry, who was 4F. But a lot of the time when Grandma Dora wasn't sick she would fill up the places with soldiers from Camp Campbell and that was nice. The soldiers would let the children wear their soldier hats, and one gave Lee Ann a shiny button that said US on it. He said that it meant "us" because she had won his heart forever. He was teasing because she knew what US meant.

After dinner the grown-ups would start to talk about something called 'the situation,' and that meant it was time for all the children to go in the hall and play jacks. Sometimes Lee Ann would slip back in the dining room and crawl under the table to hear about 'the situation.' When Grandma Dora would spot her she'd say, "Sha! *Die Kinder!*" and everyone would stop talking. Then she would say, "Leah Chana, why don't you go back and play with the other children." She never called her Lee Ann, only Leah Chana, because that was her mama's name who died right after they came from Russia while she was having Uncle Simon, because things were bad then. Lee Ann never did get to hear too much about 'the situation,' except that it was even worse being a little Jewish girl in Europe than it was in West Nashville.

On Sundays they would go to Grandma Pearl and Papa Ben's for lunch. Uncle Alfred's wife, Aunt Carolyn, would be there with the twins, Danny and Sara Jean. Little Bubbie would be there too.

Little Bubbie was Papa Ben's mama, and she was so old that she had started growing down instead of up. She was even older than Grandlady. She talked funny because she grew up in Russia and never learned to talk American real well, and her voice sounded like a frog. She was always wanting to kiss the children, but she had whiskers, and they'd try to get out of it whenever they could. They figured she couldn't shave because she was a woman.

Danny and Sara Jean were seven, a little older than Lee Ann, and a lot more fun to play with than Lori Sue, who was only three. Danny would get kind of uppity because he was a boy, but all Sara Jean and Lee Ann had to do was say the words, "the Big Toe," and that would shut him up. Reason was that, usually after lunch, when they finished helping Grandma Pearl take the plates into the kitchen, Danny, Sara Jean and Lee Ann would go next door to see Mr. Collins. He drove a train for the L and N railroad and loved to tell stories. One day in particular, he told them this story about the Big Toe. Now the Big Toe wasn't a regular toe. It was real big, and it didn't have any body connected to it, and it could do whatever it wanted to; mainly it wanted to scare people, like the time these two children named Billy and Susie had to stay home by themselves because their mama and daddy had to go out, and it was raining real hard and storming, and they were in bed and they heard this thump, thump, thump, and Billy said, "Don't worry it's only a branch hitting the roof." But it kept on thumping and they could hear it coming up the stairs, and they slammed their door and locked it, but it came right up to the bedroom door and started banging on it and banged so hard that all of a sudden it made this hole in the door and the children saw this Big Toe sticking out, and if their mama and daddy hadn't come home in the nick of time, no telling what would have happened.

That day, on the way back to Grandma Pearl's, they were talking about the Big Toe and how scary it was and all, and Danny started saying things like girls are sissies and boys don't get scared, and making Sara Jean and Lee Ann feel lowly.

Anyway, when they got back, Aunt Carolyn was sitting on the porch and she said, "How would you like to go for ice cream?" And they all said they sure would.

Aunt Carolyn said, "Sit right here on the steps and I'll go in and get Lori Sue and my car keys."

Well, Sara Jean and Lee Ann sat down like they were supposed to, but Danny started toward the car. He had just put his hand on the door handle, when they heard a loud froglike voice coming from inside the car.

"Getz in de car," it said.

Danny let go that handle like it was electrified and started running back to the house. Every hair on that boy's head stood straight up. Then Sara Jean and Lee Ann saw Little Bubbie peeping through the car window, and they got the giggles so bad they both wet their pants.

That summer went on and on and it got hotter and hotter. Lori Sue's bottom was all covered in little red heat bumps. Every day Mama would come home for lunch and there was no letter from Daddy. It was too hot to play outside, so Lee Ann just stayed in the house. She had gotten out her box of letters from Daddy and read them so many times that they were getting all raggedy.

Sometimes she'd go in the kitchen and help Ada shell butter beans and play with the little red ration tokens they used to buy food.

Sometimes Ada would say, "Don't yo feel good, Sugar?" and sometimes she would say, "Maybe yo need a tonic to pep yo up."

Then one evening, when she was drying the girls off after their bath, Ada said, "Yo two have shore been good girls, so Ada's gonna give yo a treat. Tomorrow afernoon we gonna go downtown to the Loews Picture Show."

Lee Ann was all naked and dripping wet, but she threw her towel down and hugged Ada around the neck.

"Slow down, Chile, yo gettin' Ada all wet."

"Lori Sue Baby, we're going to the picture show," Lee Ann said and hugged her, too.

That night when she got into bed she thought about the other time she had gone to the picture show. Aunt Sylvia had taken her. Mama drove them downtown and let them off in front of the Loews Theater. Aunt Sylvia walked right up to the lady in the booth and bought two tickets, and then, almost as soon as she got them, she gave them to this man in a gold and red uniform who tore them up. Lee Ann whispered to Aunt Sylvia that she didn't think that was very nice, but Aunt Sylvia said that's what they do there. They walked down this long, long hall that had a red velvet rope running down the middle, so that people coming in and people going out wouldn't get mixed up. All along the sides of the hall were giant-sized photographs of movie stars, the same ones that were in Aunt Sylvia's movie magazines. At the end of the hall was a big counter with a popcorn machine and more candy than Lee Ann had ever seen...even in Hill's Grocery.

Aunt Sylvia bought her some popcorn that had just come hot out of the popper and a box of Milkduds, and they went inside. It was hard to find a seat because it was so dark, but a man with a flashlight helped them. Then the screen lit up and first off was a big lion that looked out and roared, and Lee Ann hid her face in Aunt Sylvia's lap and said she wanted to go home. But Aunt Sylvia said that part would be over in a minute and it was.

That was the only thing that worried Lee Ann about going to the picture show...that lion. All the next morning she was fidgety because it was taking so long to be afternoon. But finally Ada said, "It's time to get dressed now."

Lee Ann put on her navy blue dress with the big white collar, and Ada dressed Lori Sue in her yellow outfit with the white pinafore. While Lee Ann was helping Lori Sue put on her Mary Jane shoes, Ada went to the basement and put on her good print dress and her shiny black hat.

Mrs. Burton and Katy were outside watering the grass. Lee Ann waved to Katy. She was about to wave back, when Mrs. Burton jerked her hand down and pushed her toward the house. But Lee Ann didn't care. They looked so good all dressed up. She was proud for the neighbors to see them as they walked to the bus stop.

She held Lori Sue's hand and told her to be a big girl and behave herself, because they were going to ride on a bus for the very first time. When the bus came, Ada boosted them up the high step and dropped some coins into a glass box beside the driver. They clinked and clattered as they slid down the chute and disappeared. Lee Ann reckoned that must be what Ada called bus fare.

Ada showed them where to sit, and Lee Ann scooted across the seat first because she wanted to sit next to the window. Ada stood in the aisle next to them. Lee Ann was looking out the window trying to catch a glimpse of their store on Charlotte Pike when she heard the man's voice.

"What do you think you are doing, Nigger," he shouted. "Get to the back of the bus where you belong."

Lee Ann slid over closer to Lori Sue and looked up at Ada. She was standing there kind of straight and still, and she said in a quiet voice, "I'm sorry, suh, but I'm tendin' to these chillun."

When Lee Ann saw the man raise up the big black umbrella he was carrying, she grabbed on to Lori Sue. She could feel Lori Sue's little heart going a mile a minute.

In the meanest voice she ever heard, the man said, "Do what I say, Nigger!"

Ada reached down, scooped them up in both arms, and carried them to the back of the bus. It was packed with colored folks, but they squeezed together and made room for Ada. Ada held Lori Sue on her lap and another lady held Lee Ann. Lee Ann was trembling, so the lady put her big arms around her and held her close.

Lee Ann leaned over and whispered, "Ada, why..."

"Hush, Chile," she said, "jest hush now."

So she sat there real quiet while the bus went through Shucker Town where the colored folks lived, past Papa Ben's store, and climbed up the hill by the State Capitol. When they got to Church Street, Ada reached over and dinged the bell. Lee Ann gave a quick look down the aisle as they got off the bus. The man was gone.

Ada stopped to look in Castner's window, and Lee Ann asked if they could go in and see Aunt Sylvia, but Ada said they better not, maybe on the way back. They crossed the street to the Loews Theater, and Lee Ann pulled Ada toward the ticket booth.

"No thisaway, honey," Ada said and started around the side of the building.

Church Street — Downtown Nashville — 1940's

Lee Ann was sure Ada was wrong, but she wasn't about to make any more trouble. They went down this alley in between two tall buildings, and even though it was a sunny day, the alley was so dark that she had to blink her eyes to see. There was a rotten smell in the alley, and when Lee Ann accidentally bumped against a trash can, a small animal ran out. Ada stopped halfway down and opened her purse. It was then that Lee Ann noticed the cut out place on the side of the building and the colored woman sitting behind the glass window. Ada bought three tickets and opened the metal door alongside the window.

The door made a screeching noise that sounded like the one on "The Inner Sanctum" and Lee Ann said, "Ada, I'm scared."

Lori Sue squeezed Lee Ann's hand so hard the blood went out of it.

Ada said, "It's all right, sugar."

There was a wooden staircase inside lit by one bare light bulb. Since there wasn't anyone to tear up their tickets, they started climbing up the wooden stairs. Each step made a creaking sound and they seemed to go on forever. Ada carried Lori Sue, but Lee Ann had to walk and her legs began to ache.

She knew they were getting near the top because she could hear voices. They walked into a room at the tippy top of the building and sat down on a long wooden bench. A few colored folks were already sitting in there and they nodded to Ada. She nodded back. Way, way down Lee Ann could see a tiny screen, but it made her dizzy to look, so she leaned her head against Ada's arm. She fell asleep and dreamed of lions, black umbrellas, wooden legs, mean-eyed people and bombs bursting in air.

RETURN

❦ 1945 ❧

Lee Ann had been looking forward to her eighth birthday with great anticipation. Her mother Rosalyn knew that. Rosalyn had promised Lee Ann a most wonderful day. She would take her to the Belle Meade Theater to see Walt Disney's *Cinderella* and then out to dinner at a restaurant afterwards. That's what she told Lee Ann, but actually she was planning a surprise birthday party. The birthday fell on Sunday, which was fortuitous because it was the one day of the week that Rosalyn wasn't working. The rest of the week, she spent long hours at the suburban department store that her husband, George, had established in West Nashville. With George in the service, fighting in the Pacific, their lives had been turned upside down. Now instead of being a housewife, Rosalyn was trying to hold the business together until he came back. She had little time to spend with her two young daughters, Lee Ann and Lori Sue.

Rosalyn and her sister, Sylvia, who was living with the family while George was gone, had worked all week on the party preparations. Every evening, after they listened to the ten o'clock news on the big radio in the living room, they would busy themselves with plans for the party. It was a welcome distraction from the realities of the war and the responsibilities of everyday life. They spent hours wrapping party favors, practicing dropping clothes pins into a milk bottle, drawing a donkey and twenty tails for *Pin the Tail on the Donkey*, planning the cake, and a myriad of other preparations.

The party couldn't be held at home because it was to be a

surprise. So Rosalyn's mother, Dora, had agreed to have it at her house. The twenty invitations had been mailed. All the children in the extended family had been invited, as well as those of close friends. They had plotted the timing so that the children would be in place before Rosalyn, Lee Ann and Lori Sue arrived. Sylvia would go to her mother's earlier and oversee the arrangements.

It never occurred to Rosalyn that this would present a problem. But then she hadn't figured Lee Ann into the equation. Rosalyn, who was a people person, adaptable and kind, never really could fathom Lee Ann, who was single-minded, intense and passionate. Lee Ann, who could spend hours alone with her books, who analyzed and strategized, was a bit of a mystery to her mother.

Bathed, dressed in her new yellow party dress and wearing a big yellow bow in her brown hair, Lee Ann looked angelic as she got into the car beside her little sister, Lori Sue.

"We're stopping by Grandma Dora's on the way. She wants to wish you a happy birthday," Rosalyn called to the girls in the back seat.

"I don't want to go," whined Lee Ann.

"We'll just stop for a minute, run in."

"No!"

"Lee Ann, be nice. You're eight years old and not a baby anymore."

"I'm not a baby," chimed in the five-year-old Lori Sue.

"No, of course, you're not," said Rosalyn wearily.

"You're turning into Grandma Dora's street," squealed Lee Ann.

"Yes, I am. I told her we were coming and we are."

"Not me, you two can go in, but I'm staying in the car. I'm ready to go to the picture show."

"Come on, Lee Ann," said Rosalyn as she opened the door to the back seat.

"No!"

"Look, Lori Sue and I are going in. If you don't follow us in two minutes, there is going to be big trouble."

"But it's *my* birthday," pouted Lee Ann.

When Rosalyn and Lori Sue got inside, they found that Sylvia had the twenty little party guests hidden behind the French doors leading into the dining room.

"Where's Lee Ann?" asked Sylvia and Dora almost in the same breath.

"She won't get out of the car."

"She's being a bad girl," confided Lori Sue.

"Don't worry, I'll get her," said Sylvia. She poked her head behind the French doors. "You kids know what to do." She started out.

"Hello, darling. Happy Birthday! Do you have a kiss for Aunt Sylvia? I have a special present for you inside. Please come in and get it."

Lee Ann gave her aunt a kiss and hug and reluctantly climbed out of the car. As they stepped into the living room, twenty children jumped out from behind the French doors singing *Happy Birthday*. Lee Ann burst into tears.

The party was a great success. The party favors were given out; the pins dropped into the milk bottle; the tails pinned on the donkey; and the cake eaten. Everyone had had a grand time. That is everyone except Lee Ann. Nothing seemed to jolt Lee Ann out of her funk — not even Aunt Sylvia's promise to take her to the movie next Sunday, nor the car full of birthday presents.

It was only after they got home, exhausted and out of sorts, that Lee Ann got the best birthday present of all. There was a telegram waiting for them. Her daddy was coming home.

Everything changed in the Blumberg household when George

Blumberg returned. Sylvia moved out, Rosalyn stopped going to the store weekdays, and there was once again a man in the house. To Lori Sue, he was a stranger, but it took little time for Lee Ann to readjust to the father she adored. Except for the limp from the leg wound he received during a bombing attack, he seemed just the same to her. Every evening after the girls had their baths and were ready for bed, he would pile them into the big double bed he and Rosalyn shared — Lee Ann on one side and Lori Sue on the other — and create another story of the continuing adventures of Krazy Kat.

Even Ada Baugh, their nursemaid and housekeeper, who had come to care for the children while George was away, felt the impact of the change. The family had been concerned that George and Ada might not hit it off. But right from the beginning he began bringing Ada little things from the store, a pair of earrings, a new straw hat, and they got on fine. Sometimes when Ada was working in the kitchen, he would sneak up and untie her apron strings and Ada would say, "Now you go on, Mr. George!" But the little smile that crept into her face revealed her pleasure.

The bond between Lee Ann and George, so rapidly reestablished, continued to grow. She begged to go to the store with him. She learned how to attach the pin tickets without sticking her fingers. She learned the pricing code. She learned how many green stamps went with a purchase. She loved the smell of the oil they rolled on the wood floors each week. She could replace the spools of thread with the correct color. She knew under which counter the cotton batting was kept and would crawl on top for a nap when she got sleepy. Best of all she liked to go with George to the corner of the basement where he had his drawing table. She'd watch as he dipped the big brushes into the tempera paints and in broad strokes write the words SALE or SPECIAL or TODAY ONLY in bold colors on big sheets of poster board.

If she were lucky, he would take her with him on his Sunday treks downtown to the Andrew Jackson Hotel, where the various

The Andrew Jackson Hotel — 6th and Deaderick — 1925-1971

salesmen set up their sample rooms. George would put the top down on his blue Oldsmobile convertible, set Lee Ann in the front seat beside him, put the car in gear and head downtown, the two of them singing *I'm Forever Blowing Bubbles* at the top of their lungs.

Lee Ann thought the Andrew Jackson was the grandest place she had ever seen. Holding each other's hands tight, they would walk through the revolving doors together, their heels clicking on the marble floor. The doors to the golden elevator would open, and the operator in his red uniform with the gold braid would greet them with a big smile and show off his gold tooth.

No matter how often she went, she was always startled when the elevator doors reopened to reveal the long dark hallway with its stained carpet and smoky smell. "We are looking for room number 432," George would say and then let Lee Ann race up and down the hall until she found it. Inside, the rooms all seemed alike. The salesmen would be surrounded by racks of ladies dresses or little girls' dresses or men's suits. Against the windows would be a folding table and chairs. On one corner of the table in a neat stack were the order blanks and a glass full of freshly sharpened pencils. Through the connecting door Lee Ann could see the bedroom where the salesmen slept.

Lee Ann liked the salesmen. They had different names and different faces, but in other ways they were all very much alike. They were outgoing, jolly, and a little travel-worn, as evidenced by the stains on their ties and the cigarette ash smudges on their shirt cuffs. They always seemed glad to see Lee Ann, setting her on their knees, giving her chewing gum and candy, and showing her pictures of their children back in New York or St. Louis or Atlanta. George would look through the racks, feel the material, and decide what he wanted. Then they would talk about price. Lee Ann understood little of what was being said — three dozen of this, a gross of that. It was the cadence of their speech that intrigued her. They would banter back and forth, until finally George would slap his hand down on the table and say, "It's a deal." Then Lee Ann knew it was time to go.

Lee Ann liked to watch George do things around the house, too. Rosalyn would make little lists for him — fix the glider on the front porch; put a new wheel on Lori Sue's tricycle; paint the lawn furniture. He even laid a wide plank across the ditch that cut through their backyard so that Lee Ann could go across to visit her friend, Janie Marie, in the winter when the ditch was full of water. She and Janie Marie would tiptoe back and forth across the plank pretending they were in the circus.

Throughout the summer, when the ditch was dry, Lee Ann and Janie Marie would scavenge it, collecting little treasures left in the wake of the winter rains. They put them in a big cardboard box in the garage. On rainy days they would gather up their loot and take it in to Ada Baugh. In Ada's capable hands the bottle caps became necklaces; the milk bottles penny banks; the tin can a toy truck.

"How'd you learn to make all this?" Lee Ann asked her.

"Honey, when yo grow up on a dirt farm in Al'bama, yo learn real quick how to do for yoself."

"What was it like on that farm, Ada?"

"Ain't nothin' yo'd want to hear 'bout, Chile."

"Were you slaves?"

Ada threw her head back and gave one of her deep laughs that started way down in her throat. "No, honey, we wuz free...just barely."

"What does free mean?"

"Lord, Chile, I don't know where they got yo. Yo can aks the most persnickety questions. Free means...it means...bein' able to make yo own decisions, I reckon."

Not long after George returned, he and Rosalyn started talking about a new house. They told the clerks at the store it was because they wanted each girl to have a room of her own. But uppermost in their minds was getting the girls out of West Nashville. They had liked the convenience of living only a few blocks from the store. It had simplified life for Rosalyn while George was away, but now that George was back and the girls were growing up, they wanted to be in an area with more Jewish people.

No new houses had been built during the war and the housing market in Nashville was tight. They felt very lucky to find the house in Richland Park, the neighborhood where Rosalyn had grown up. It was a 1930's house with large rooms and an attic they could refinish as a playroom for the girls.

They moved in March but decided to let Lee Ann finish out the school year at Sylvan Park School. It was a short bus ride from the school to their new home, and they approached Lee Ann with the idea of riding the bus home from school. George would drop her off in the mornings on the way to the store, and when Rosalyn wasn't available to pick her up, Lee Ann could ride the bus. Lee Ann was delighted with the idea.

For the first few weeks after the move, Rosalyn picked her up every day. But about a month after the move, Rosalyn was driving to Kentucky to spend the day with her cousin, Becky Greenberg, and Lee Ann was to take the bus home. Rosalyn carefully reminded Lee Ann of the exact procedure — how to walk the two blocks to the bus stop; where to stand at the bus stop; how much money to put in the coin box; how and when to pull the cord to let the driver know where to stop; and where to get off. She admonished her to wear her mittens and her new wool coat and leggings, as it was a cold March day, and she might have to wait a half hour for the bus.

Lee Ann could hardly wait for the dismissal bell to ring. She filled her book satchel hurriedly, pulled on the leggings, then her coat and mittens. She had brought earmuffs as well. Appropriately bundled, she headed for the front entrance and down the broad steps to the street. Waves of children walked past, splitting off to go their various ways. Lee Ann continued straight ahead, until she reached Murphy Road. There were already several children milling around the bus stop and soon others joined them. Two children from the sixth grade, twelve-year olds, began looking Lee Ann up and down. They looked at her leggings and snickered.

"What in the world are them things," they shouted.

"Leggings," Lee Ann replied in a voice so low it was barely audible.

"I do believe that's the Jew Baby," called out one.

"Jew Baby, Jew Baby, Jew Baby," she chanted, and the others quickly joined in.

Someone pulled Lee Ann's book satchel off her shoulder, and as she reached for it, someone else pulled her earmuffs off.

"Do you believe in Jesus Christ?"

Lee Ann nodded her head, yes.

The dirt at the bus stop, damp from the winter rains, had turned into mud, under all those feet. Lee Ann, lunging for her belongings, lost her footing and slid into the mud; the circle around her tightened. The children continued circling and taunting. Too frightened to cry or call out, she lay in the mud and it was only when the bus pulled up that the crowd dispersed.

Lee Ann got up, grabbed her satchel and earmuffs, and started running back to the school. The bus driver honked at her, but she kept running. Now, as the horror set in, the tears began to flow, making muddy streaks down her cheeks. She was out of breath as she climbed the steps to the door. She pulled the handle, but it was locked. She began pounding on the glass, then slid down in a heap.

Her heart jumped when she heard the key turning in the lock. The cleaning lady opened the door and looked down at Lee Ann. "Lord," she said, "What done happened to yo, Chile?"

Lee Ann ran to her, threw her arms around her legs, buried her head in her skirt and began to sob loudly. The woman lifted her up and took her into the principal's office. Everyone was gone. She sat Lee Ann in the principal's wooden armchair and pulled several sheets of tissue from a box on the desk. She took them to the hand basin and dampened them. When she came back, she removed Lee Ann's coat and leggings and began wiping her with the tissues. There was blood on Lee Ann's lip where she had cut it falling. It had begun to throb.

Under the gentle touch of this kind lady, Lee Ann calmed down, her tears stopped flowing.

"What's yo name, Chile?"

"Lee Ann."

"What happened out thar?"

"I was waiting for the bus, and the big kids pushed me around and pulled off my book satchel. I fell in the mud and they wouldn't let me get up. They were calling me names."

"Lord, in Heaven! Why would anyone want to do sech a terrible thang to a pretty little white girl like you?"

"I'm not white," Lee Ann protested, sobbing. "I'm Jewish."

"Oh," the black woman said, and two hundred years of pain welled up in her eyes. "Do yo know how to use the telephone? Can you call yo mama?"

"She's not home. I better call my daddy."

After George heard the story and thanked the lady, he and Lee Ann climbed into the Oldsmobile. On the way home George was silent, they didn't sing, they didn't even talk. His jaw was set, his face red. He kept glancing at Lee Ann but didn't speak. When they arrived home, he asked Ada to give her a bath. "She's had a bad experience," he said. "Fix her a nice treat afterwards."

After her bath, sitting in her bathrobe in the kitchen with a glass of milk and some of Ada's good oatmeal cookies, she could hear voices in the living room and realized her mother had gotten home. She moved over to the door so she could hear what was being said.

"Oh, George, I'm so sorry. Poor Lee Ann!"

"You should be sorry, Rosalyn. I begged you to take her out of that school."

"But, George, she only had three months left. I thought her schoolwork might suffer. So many adjustments to make."

"I cannot believe this! I was over in the Pacific for two years. What was I fighting for? To make the world a safer place for our wives and children. That's a joke. Everyone, even the rednecks in West Nashville, know what the Nazis did to our people, our children. Where does it come from, this hatred? A sweet, innocent little girl like Lee Ann, who never hurt anyone. Why?"

"I don't know, George, probably no one knows. It's not logical. It doesn't fit reality. But it's always there. People need someone to pick on, to put down. The coloreds are an easy target and so are we."

"Well, what are we going to do about it?'

"I'll go over to the school in the morning and speak to the principal. We'll get her transferred tomorrow."

"Are you going to take Lee Ann?"

"I think so. Don't you think it's important for her to know that when something bad happens we can't just run away, put it totally out of our mind; it always comes back to haunt us."

"Mama, do I have to go?"

"You don't have to stay, honey. We are just going to see Mr. Carlson, the principal. He really wants you to come, so he can talk to you."

Lee Ann sat somber-faced all the way to the school. As they passed the bus stop, she looked away. Inside, Rosalyn and Lee Ann met with the principal, and Lee Ann once again related what had happened the day before.

"Do you know the names of any of the children involved?" Mr. Carlson asked.

"No."

"Would you recognize them if you saw them again?"

"Yes."

"Come with me."

He took Lee Ann by the hand and Rosalyn followed. They walked up to the second floor, where the older grades met, and stopped outside a classroom door.

"Lee Ann, we will go inside, and I want you to identify anyone you recognize."

"Is this really necessary?" protested Rosalyn.

"It's the only way I know to nip it in the bud."

They walked into the classroom. Mr. Carlson went over and briefly spoke with the teacher, then brought Lee Ann to the front of the class.

"Okay, Lee Ann, see if you recognize anyone."

She studied the staring, puzzled faces row by row until finally, in the last row, she recognized the two ring leaders.

"There," she said. "Those two in the back." The room began slowly spinning, and Lee Ann felt the nausea rising from the bottom of her stomach. She rushed from the room but couldn't make it to the bathroom before her breakfast landed on the floor in front of her. Rosalyn was right behind her, with Mr. Carlson following.

Rosalyn turned and glared at the principal. She reached in her purse and pulled out a handkerchief and began wiping Lee Ann's face.

"Look what you've done!" she screamed at him, as she picked Lee Ann up and started down the stairs.

She broke all speed limits on the way home and rushed into the house with Lee Ann. When Ada came through the kitchen doors, both Rosalyn and Lee Ann burst into tears.

"Lord, Miz Rosalyn, what done happened? I'z gonna call Mr. George right now!"

"No, Ada, don't do that. It will only get him upset, too. And Heaven knows, he's been through enough already. I'll tell you what," Rosalyn added, "why don't you make us some of that good hot chocolate? It'll calm our nerves."

Rosalyn put down her purse, took off her coat, then helped Lee Ann out of hers.

"Sit down, honey," she said to Lee Ann, as she crossed over to the bookshelf and reached up.

"I saved this brand-new paperdoll book for a rainy day. I think today surely qualifies, don't you? I'll go get the scissors. You're going to love this book, Lee Ann."

ELLIS

❧ 1950 ❧

The dog next door let out a long, agonized howl, as he did every time an ambulance passed. It was this concert, the siren of the ambulance and the wailing of the dog, that woke Ellis. He rolled over and looked at the clock on the night table. Six o'clock. He hoisted himself up and sat on the edge of the bed for a moment, twisting his head from side to side to clear his mind.

It was getting harder and harder to get going in the morning. But he smiled as he remembered last night and the pretty young co-ed from Tennessee State.

Ellis Brown was forty-nine years old, divorced and held three jobs. At night he was the bouncer at the New Era Club on Cedar Street, and during the day he alternated between the being the houseman for Mr. Samuel Marlowe and driving Miz Reba Marlowe, Mr. Samuel's mother.

He hurriedly showered and dressed in his black trousers, white shirt and black tie. Putting his chauffeur's cap on his head, he locked the door to his small house in North Nashville and got into the 1940 black Cadillac sedan parked in his driveway, a gift from Mr. Samuel Marlowe.

Miss Fanny Mae was already waiting at the end of her driveway when he arrived at few minutes later. She was a heavy-set, cocoa-colored woman about his own age. She was dressed in her white uniform and white oxfords, with a white starched cap on her head. She did the cooking for the Marlowe family and kept the first floor clean. It was Miss Fanny Mae with whom Ellis worked most closely.

She made out his work schedule for the house — when to wax the furniture; when to polish the silver; when to wash the chandelier prisms. Ellis had his own time schedule for pressing Mr. Samuel's suits and washing the cars. He didn't do yard work. James Doaks came twice a week to mow the lawn and tend the garden.

With Miss Fanny Mae and her bulk comfortably arranged in the back seat, Ellis headed down 16th to pick up Elvira, the laundress and upstairs maid. Elvira, whose primary goal in life was to reach that great white mansion in the sky and wash the clothes of Jesus Christ himself, did not approve of Ellis and his profane life style. Ellis knew this and consequently dismissed Elvira as a skinny, hymn-singing know-it-all. Still, she was one of his riders, and he had to be somewhat civil to her.

Ellis retraced his route back to Cedar, then over to West End, and then down Belle Meade Blvd. Every morning the black neighborhoods of North Nashville would empty out, their occupants heading by bus or car to service the wealthy white communities in the western part of the city.

Ellis pulled around back of the large English Tudor home of the Marlowe family. Set amid five acres of mostly wooded area, the house itself was surrounded by an English garden filled with late summer roses. The servants climbed up the steps leading to the kitchen door. Fanny Mae hurried inside, grabbed her apron and began preparations for breakfast, the help first and then the family.

Elvira headed for the servants' quarters over the garage to sort the ironing, and as Ellis started for his room in the basement, Fanny Mae called out: "Ellis, don't forget the big party next week. Miz Florence sez some mighty fine folks gwanna be here 'cluding the Guvner. I got me a whole list fer yo."

Ellis turned around. "Is they going out ter the farm this weekend?"

"Lord, no, too much to do. Getting ready for the party. And Mr. David's comin' home Saturday. They want to meet his train."

Ellis continued down the unpainted wooden steps, past the laundry and the storage room with its cases of canned goods and boxes of cleaning products, until he reached the small alcove in the back that was his haven. He took off his cap and hung it on a wooden peg, then sat on the narrow cot and changed from his regular shoes to the black highly polished ones he kept at work.

The thought of David coming home excited him. He liked a house with children in it. Young Mr. Samuel, Sim, was now old enough to work in the mill during the summer. And with David away at summer camp, the house was empty of young people during the day, and it made Ellis sad. David was Ellis's favorite. He was only six-years old when Ellis came to work for the Marlowes and, over the years, Ellis had become a kind of surrogate father to him — teaching him how to ride a bike, hit a baseball, wash the car and change the oil, driving him to school and to the ballgames. Mr. Sim had already been away at prep school in Connecticut, and then he was in college and hadn't really needed Ellis that much.

"Ellis, breakfast!" Fanny Mae called down.

Elvira was already seated at the kitchen table. In front of her, heaped on a plate, was a stack of corn cakes, two strips of bacon, and a fried egg. Ellis pulled out a chair at the far end of the table and sat down.

"Whatcha want Ellis? I have grits and gravy, too."

The two ate silently while Fannie Mae kept up a flow of food and family gossip. Miz Reba's gall bladder is actin' up again; Mr. Samuel and Miz Florence are plannin' a trip to Paris; Mr. Antonio, the fruit and vegetable man, is only gonna deliver on Thursdays from now on; James Doaks hurt his back, so he's sendin' his son, Will, to do the yard this week; Miz Florence can't decide whether to hire parkers for the party — would people be drivin' themselves or have drivers; Mr. David's goin' to a new school this year — that Montgomery Bell 'cademy — you know the place, Ellis? On West End? Miz Reba wants the card table set up in the sunroom this afternoon for her bridge game. She sez the 'girls' can see better in there.

"Yawl finish up now. Iz got to get to fixing for the fam'ly."

A half hour later, the table was set in the sunny breakfast room — an embroidered tablecloth, white on white — china and crystal — and a small vase of roses from the garden in the center.

Samuel Marlowe and his wife, Florence, came down the stairway first and waited while Reba, Samuel's mother, descended slowly, seated in the elevator chair that ran down the side of the staircase. Samuel took his mother's arm and helped her into the breakfast room.

Ellis removed the starched white cloth jacket from its peg in the pantry and put it on. He folded the morning paper and tucked it under his arm. Fannie Mae poured freshly squeezed orange juice into a silver pitcher, then handed it to Ellis and watched him go though the swinging door into the breakfast room.

He placed the paper in front of Mr. Samuel who said, "Morning, Ellis. Can you come into the library after breakfast, I need to speak with you."

"Yessuh," said Ellis, as he poured the juice and continued around the table.

"None for me, Ellis," said Reba "I'm being careful."

Later when the dishes had been cleared away, Ellis knocked on the library door. He was always uneasy in that room with its dark wood paneling and floor to ceiling shelves full of books. It was Mr. Samuel's room and Ellis was uneasy with him, too.

"Come in, Ellis. Take a seat."

Mr. Samuel was seated behind his desk, and Ellis sat down in one of the chair across from him.

"I'll get right to it, Ellis. You know I run a big company. Marlowe Milling has over 1000 employees. I am a fair man. We've never had a union. The employees never needed one. I am fair, but I also expect a day's work out of everyone. It's the way I was brought up. I, myself, adhere to that principle. I rarely leave the mill on a work day. I never take off an afternoon and play golf like some of my friends. I'm there from 8:30 to 6:30 every day and only take a two week vacation each year. I expect my employees to follow my example."

"Yessuh."

"Now, Ellis, you and I have talked in the past about your work ethic and your life style. I have given you ample warning. Nothing seems to have changed. You come in and piddle around dusting, and unless my mother needs you to drive, spend most of the day dozing on that cot of yours down in the basement."

"I gets tired, Suh."

"Of course, you do. Anyone who is up half the night carousing is tired the next day. I've asked you to quit that job at the New Era. I even offered you more pay if you would. But now I'm fed up. I'm going to have to let you go."

Samuel Marlowe opened his large checkbook and quickly wrote out two checks. He handed them to Ellis.

"This one is your regular weekly pay, and this other one is one month's severance pay. You can keep the car. I think that's fair, Ellis. So, after dinner tonight, you can gather up your things. I will give you a reference, even though I'm not comfortable with it. I'm sorry it has come to this. I know the family will not be happy with my decision, especially David, but I have no recourse."

"Yessuh."

So that was it, Ellis thought, Mr. Samuel was letting him go. Go where? This was his family — Miz Reba, Miz Florence, Mr. Sim, and David. He had promised to teach David how to drive an automobile this fall. And Miz Reba. Who was going to go get her prescriptions for her? And who would make sure she took the right medicine at the right time? He wouldn't get to see Mr. Sim and Miz Sally get married. He'd never taste Miz Fanny Mae's biscuits and red eye gravy again or smell her fried chicken cooking.

Ellis sat on the cot and looked down at the two checks in his hand, then up at the photographs he had taped to the wall: Mr. David when he was seven with his front tooth missing; Mr. Sim with David on his shoulders at the Woodmont pool; Mr. Sim with his high school diploma in his black cap and gown; Miz Reba at her 80th birthday party in that blue dress that she loved so much; Mr. Samuel and Miz Florence in a gondola in Italy.

His body felt like lead. When the buzzer from upstairs rang, he wasn't sure that he could actually stand up. It was Miz Reba's buzzer. He hoisted himself up. What I need right now is a stiff drink, he thought. But he never brought liquor to work with him.

He walked through the rest of the day in a daze like a man in bereavement. He took down the photos and packed them in a small suit case Miz Elvira had found for him. He put in his shiny shoes, his two white jackets, his extra black bow tie and extra black socks, and the ashtray that David had made him at camp. On the way home, Miz Fannie Mae cried, but Miz Elvira just couldn't resist an "I told you so."

"You fired Ellis?! Daddy, how could you? Grandma Reba's up in her room crying her eyes out, and when David gets home tomorrow, it'll be hell to pay."

"I don't need your criticism, Sim. I've got too much on my mind right now with this affair tonight. I didn't have any choice. Sometimes you just have to bite the bullet, son."

"Who's going to drive Grandma Reba?"

"I've hired a fellow. Thomas Burrows is his name. Came highly recommended. He's a married man and a churchgoer. He starts Monday."

On the whole, David liked summer camp. He liked the Wisconsin forests and lakes. He liked the camaraderie and the competition with the other boys. What he despised was the silly rules and routines. After two months of it, he had had his fill and looked forward to coming home. He never imagined that Ellis would be gone.

Samuel had known that David would be upset. He had braced himself for the onslaught, but it never came. On the contrary, David didn't say a word. He just glared. David's silence disturbed Samuel, but in a way he welcomed it. Samuel was a firm believer in civility. One didn't raise one's voice; parents didn't disagree in front of the children; one didn't show raw emotion; everything could be worked out peaceably with logic and understanding. It was the way he was raised, the way he was raising his children. Still David was the most emotional, the most volatile member of the household, and his silence was a puzzlement.

David may have given his father the silent treatment, but he poured his heart out to Fannie Mae. They spent hours in the kitchen commiserating. Fannie Mae was the line of communication between David and Ellis. Yes, he missed David; no, he hadn't found another job yet; yes, he was still working at the New Era Club.

"What are we going to do about this, Fannie Mae?"

"Ain't nothin' we can do, honey."

"Oh, yes, there is. There is always a way if you want something badly enough. You just have to think it through. Make a plan."

"What yo sayin', Chile?"

"Just that I'm thinking of a plan, that's all."

"Now don't yo go and do sumpthin' foolish, yo hear."

"Don't worry, Fannie Mae, it's all going to work out."

Thomas Burrows was delighted to get the job with the Marlowes. The pay was good and the conditions excellent. He was doing what a lifetime of training had taught him to do. He should have been a happy man, but something was going wrong.

First, it had been the bank receipt. Miz Reba had asked him to make the deposit down at the Belle Meade branch and he had. He was sure that he had left the receipt on the hall table, but when he went to get it, it wasn't there. They had looked everywhere, but it never turned up and he had to go back down to the bank and get a copy.

Then Mr. Samuel had complained that he hadn't cleaned the cigarettes out of the ashtray in the car when he washed it. But he was sure he had.

Then he had tripped while he was serving Miz Florence her after dinner coffee and spilled it on her favorite tablecloth. He still couldn't figure out what made him trip.

Then one day, when he went to put on his white jacket, there was a red stain on it, and Miz Elvira said his other one was in the washing machine.

It seemed like every day there was something else. It made Thomas nervous. He began to forget things. His hands shook when he served dinner. His wife said that maybe he was just getting old.

When Mr. Samuel called him into the library and told him things were not working out, he should have been disappointed, but he felt such a sense of relief that he almost smiled.

Samuel Marlowe was not a man who relented easily. He was a cautious man who thought things out carefully, and on the rare occasions when he did make a mistake, it pained him to admit it. Returning home that evening, he went into the library. As was his habit every evening, he would open the panel doors to the bar and pour himself a scotch and soda. With drink in hand, he walked to the foot of the stairwell and called out. "David, son, if you are up there, please come down here a minute."

A half minute later, David joined him in the library.

"Sit down, David." David sank into the down sofa while Samuel, standing, leaned against the bar. "I don't know exactly what's been going on around here and how much you've had a hand in it, but I do know that things haven't worked out as I thought they would. Your grandmother hardly speaks to me, and nobody seems very happy around here. So, in order that we may once more have peace in this family, I have decided to ask Ellis to come back. Just provisionally, you understand."

David stood up. "When?"

"Starting tomorrow morning."

"Well, Dad, under the circumstances that seems like a good decision."

When David heard the car pull into the driveway the next morning, he jumped out of bed and ran barefoot down the stairs and into the kitchen. He grabbed Ellis and hugged him as he came through the back door. They both started laughing and crying. So did Miz Fannie Mae and even, would you believe, Miz Elvira.

PEN PAL

❦ 1953 ❧

> June 10, 1998…Thomas J. Holliway, Evangelist Minister, age 64, died last night at Vanderbilt Hospital. The cause of death was listed as heart failure. Rev. Holliway was a life-long resident of Nashville. He is survived by his wife, Katherine, three children and six grandchildren. Services tomorrow at the Mt. Olivet Cemetery 2:00 P.M.

Lee Ann pushed her breakfast plate aside, pulled the newspaper closer, and read the obituary again. Tom Holliway, it has to be! Tom Holliway. Its the right name, the right age, and, thinking back, the right calling. "Its uncanny," she thought, "I almost never read these things. Why today? And why this?" She felt an unexpected tightening in her throat and a sadness that grew as her mind raced back to another time.

❖ ❖ ❖

Sept. 25, 1953
Kimpo, Korea

Dear Lee Ann,

You don't know me, but I saw your picture in the Nashville Banner last week. (We get it over here once in a while.) Anyway, you looked so nice, and the award you received from the Jewish church was so nice that I thought maybe you would agree to be a pen pal for a lonely soldier in Korea. Lucky for me, they put your name and address in the paper. I'm from Nashville, too. I am nineteen years old. I live with my mother and younger sister on Shelby Avenue in East Nashville. (That is when I am not away fighting a war.) My mother works at Marlowe Milling Company, and my sister goes to East High School. Lee Ann, I hope you will write. My address is:

A/2C Tom Holliway AF 15738962Hq.
3rd Supply Sqdn. 3rd F.I.W.
APO 920 Postmaster
San Francisco, Calif.

Sincerely Yours,
Tom Holliway

❖   ❖   ❖

Oct. 10, 1953
Nashville, Tenn.

Dear Tom Holliway,

When I went down to the mailbox and found your letter I really was confused. I mean, to get a letter from Korea! From somebody I don't even know! And why would a nineteen-year-old soldier want to write me? Naturally, I thought I better show the letter to my mother, and she showed it to Daddy. They were confused, too. Daddy said he didn't much like the idea of me writing to a stranger that nobody knew anything about, and Mama didn't cotton to the idea of me writing to a boy who wasn't Jewish. No offense, but in my family the girls don't date boys who aren't Jewish. But we all felt badly about you being lonely and way over there in Korea and Daddy said he remembered very well when he was in the army and how nice it was to get letters from home. Still, we didn't know what to do, and then Mama came up with the idea that I should ask Rabbi Friedman. So I showed him your letter (bet you never thought so many people would see that letter!) and he said that he thought it would be all right, but that some ground rules should be set down from the very beginning, so these are the rules:

1. You have to know that this is just a pen pal relationship and nothing more.
2. You must never try to call or see me when you get back.
3. The letters shouldn't get too personal, just be about things of general interest like what is happening in Nashville, how the Vols are doing and stuff like that, and you can write all about how things are in Korea.

Is that okay with you?

You already know my name and where I live. I am fifteen years old and a sophomore at West End High School. I like dramatics and public speaking. I'm in the Honor Society, the Quill and Scroll, the Latin Club and am going out for cheerleader in the Spring. I also like to work on the West Wind (the school newspaper). My other activities include being the treasurer of B'nai B'rith Girls and Asst. Sunday School teacher. That sounds like a lot, doesn't it? My mother thinks I overdo everything, but I guess that's just the way I am. I live with my mother and father and younger sister, Lori Sue. She's twelve and kind of a pest right now. I hope she'll grow out of it. I like to watch baseball and basketball games, but I'm not good at any sport (uncoordinated) and I can't carry a tune, so I can never be in any musicals, which I would dearly love to do. I sometimes think that I would like to be a movie star, but not being able to sing is a problem. I would also like to be a doctor, but being a girl, that seems an impossible dream. Oh, I also like to read. I read everything I can. I guess I'm just a romantic, because I always imagine that I am the heroine, and I try to figure out what happens after the story in the book ends.

Sincerely,
Lee Ann Blumberg

P.S. Your handwriting is beautiful. Please excuse my pitiful scrawl!

❖ ❖ ❖

Oct. 30, 1953
Kimpo, Korea

Hello, Lee Ann,

Gosh, you sure are sweet to answer such an anonymous friend. Believe me, I was amazed. The rules are fine. Since you are of a faith of a different nature, your letters will be sufficient.

Lee Ann, I will try to express to you the actions and habits of the Oriental Koreans. They exist in huts made of straw and weeds. They believe in bringing birth to earth constantly. Their occupation is strictly rice paddies. From dawn to dark they work their fields of rice. I will send you some pictures of such, as soon as I get the time. They are smart people in their way, Lee Ann. They save everything that they think may be of use. For brooms, the wild weeds that grow adequate on the hillside are bundled like a switch. Cleanness is their calling. They clean all the time. They try hard to keep their small huts neat, but this is a chore, since the household doesn't have modern conveniences. Their rooms are very insufficient.

The clothes: Just anything that will wrap around them. Mostly white. When a rexx, excuse me, when a relative passes away, they don't bury them. They put them in a wooden box like a crate and carry it to the hillside. Sit it up and leave it sitting on the ground after the ceremony. We use the dull color. They use the brightest colors to cover the body with. I will try to get a picture of this. I know it seems strange to take such a picture, so if you don't care to consult with that, please tell. The last thing I wish is to make you sore.

Church services: They form a large semi-circle in front of a table, with a cloth somewhat identical to a tarpaulin over it. Three men take part in the ceremony. What they do, I don't know. We're not supposed to participate with their religious or political activities.

Transportation: Any way to transfer the materials from place to place. The wealthy ones have carts with oxen and bicycles. The poor ones put everything on their backs. I never saw a wagon around home with as much in it as they put on their backs. Their babies are carried the same way you've seen in history books. In somewhat like a sack, attached to their backs. To keep warm, as I said earlier, they wrap anything around them, and every day many of them wait on the railroad tracks for the train to come. (Of course they get off after they see it coming.) When it passes usually fall many small particles of coal. This they grab and save until winter.

I can't think of very much at this time. But if you care to consult again with me, I'll be happy to respond as often and as prompt as possible.

In case you're interested:

1. skoshi = cheap, small, short
2. takusan = big, much, long
3. oppso = crazy
4. chotamoti = wait a minute
5. ediwa = come here
6. dyjobi = OK
7. mamsan = mother
8. papsan = daddy
9. boysan = boy
10. josan = girl

11. babysan = baby (and they are really cute too)

Did I help you any? I surely hope so.
   Your corresponding friend,

                                                  Tom

❖   ❖   ❖

Nov. 14, '53
Nashville, Tenn.

Dear Tom,

I enjoyed your letter so much! It must be very interesting to be in a
foreign country and see how other people live.. The furthest I've been
from Nashville is Florida and I love it, but it's not like going to a
foreign country. Maybe someday! I think I would like to go to places
like Paris and Rome. The only person in my family that has ever been
overseas is my daddy. He was in the Pacific during WWII, so he really
enjoyed hearing what you had to say about the life in Korea. (I didn't
let him read the letter, just told him. I have decided that it is not right
to show someone's letter to somebody else.)
   I wish that I had some interesting things to tell you, but not too
much is happening here in Nashville. The leaves on the trees were
really beautiful this year, all bright reds and golds, but they are
practically all gone (off the trees that is). They are still on the ground
and guess whose job it is to rake them? You got it! Oh, my aching
back.
   Of course, school takes up most of my time. I am taking English,
Latin II, Algebra II, Biology and World History. I like English and
Biology best and Algebra worst. I am not good at math. Daddy says
that someday I'll need it, but I can't imagine what for. Do you ever
use algebra?

The stage play "South Pacific" came to Nashville last week at the Tennessee Theater, and David and I went to see it. (David is my boyfriend.) Mary Martin wasn't in it, but it was good anyway. When I see something like that I wish I could sing. I dream about being a leading lady, but that's a joke.

There's this Jewish sorority here, and last year almost all my friends got in it, but I didn't. I haven't been able to figure out why. They have all these little black notebooks with the sorority rules in them. Secret stuff. I kind of feel left out, but it really hasn't made much of a difference. The boys still ask me out. Of course, I have a boyfriend, but my parents won't let me go steady, so I have to go out with somebody else one of the weekend nights. What we usually do is go to the movies (do you get movies over there?) or just drive around and end up at Varallo's and get chili. Unless, of course, there is a party. There are a lot of parties this year — you know, Sweet Sixteen. Most of them are really fancy — formal dresses with hoop skirts and crinolines — when you try to sit down the whole thing flops up, which can get pretty embarrassing. I'm finally getting the hang of it, but in a car it's impossible.

I've decided not to have one — a party. I'd rather save that money for something important like my college education.

What about you? How long have you been over there? And where exactly is it? I can't seem to find it on the map. What do you do all day? Is it dangerous?

Oh, by the way, my mother (the great detective) called your mother, and she's fine. They had a nice long talk. We are sending you a package, so you can look for it.

Your friend,
Lee Ann

❖　❖　❖

Dec. 5, 1953
Kimpo, Korea

Hi there, Lee Ann,

Your sweet and thoughtful letter arrived today. It made my day! It came at noon, the other four hours were easier. There isn't much to do here, so when I receive a letter, I know I can look forward to the evening and have something to occupy my miserable mind. Gee, that was a long sentence. My English is very poor, Lee, guess I didn't work hard enough in school. Not smart like you.

Say, your stationery is very nice. It goes along with your writing to me.

Lee Ann, please don't think I just want to impress upon you. I only want to show my gratitude. So send me your picture, please. One that is a real clear view of your face. I will have it painted, send it and the one you send me back to you also. I know how you feel about giving a boy that doesn't mean anything to you pictures. So as soon as I have the Korean girl paint it, I'll be sure and send it back, O.K.? Don't worry about the cost. It's my pleasure.

I envy you, Lee Ann. I'll bet being back in school is like having a birthday. It sure is a wonderful memory to me. It's another world you live in. Everything is different. Friends are real friends. Of course I can't express exactly how and why to you, because you haven't been out in the world by yourself — touring different parts, meeting different personalities, etc. But it's different over here. People seem to like me O.K. and I go along with them. You have to, to survive. But it's not like having real friends. I try to make them understand my crazy ways. (I do have peculiar ways.) My mother always says I take everything apart. I mean what people say and do. One hazard of mine is criticism. I don't like to hear a person criticize something or someone. I try not to say anything. I try to mind my own business. It seems like everything over here is so temporary. Maybe that's why everybody acts so different. All they think about is getting to Seoul. But that's not for your ears.

To answer your question, I have been here four months. Believe me, it seems like four years. But life is only what one makes it. Kimpo, Korea. Where is it? O.K. About twelve miles from Seoul, the capital. About fifteen miles from Ascom (where thirty-five thousand prisoners broke camp). We've been bombed twice since I arrived here. Thanks to God they only tore up the warehouses. Incidentally, this answers your next question. I slave at a warehouse. I receive issue and stock supplies. Ordinance! This totals ammunition, guns of different types, etc.

Please tell your sweet, thoughtful mother that I am grateful to her for the remarkable thing she did for me and Mother. May God bless her.

Your friend,
Tom

❖ ❖ ❖

Dec. 30, 1953
Miami Beach, Fla.

Dear Tom,

I bet you are surprised to get a letter on hotel stationery. We are down here for a week during vacation, and it really is fun just playing in the sun. I'm getting a kind of tan but mostly burn, because my skin is sensitive to the sun. I have to put this yukky stuff on to keep the sun out. You should see me with this white stuff on my nose. You would laugh. It helps keep the boys away and that's a relief. Believe it or not, I think I must be basically shy. I like boys one at a time, not a whole bunch buzzing around me. Hooray for zinc oxide!

Lori Sue is taking swimming lessons from this lifeguard at the hotel (you should see HIS tan), and she's turning out to be really good. She's been nicer on this trip, too.

It's great to be on vacation. December has been an unbelievable month. Did I tell you I teach a class at Sunday School? Most of the teachers are grown-ups or college students from Vanderbilt and Peabody, so it's a lot of responsibility. I am teaching drama to the grammar school-aged children, and I wrote a Chanukah play for them and directed it (first time I ever did that). Do you know anything about Chanukah? It's one of my favorite holidays (we get presents every night for eight days — not bad, huh?) Anyway , the play was about what happened on the first Chanukah — how this small group of soldiers fought off this big army and won, and all because they wanted religious freedom. I don't know how good it

Entrance to Mt. Olivet Cemetery

was, but we all had fun doing it and that's what counts. But I guess this seems kind of childish to you, what with you over there defending our country and risking your life and everything.

On top of that, I had finals just before vacation. Yuk! Then I had to work at our store (did I tell you we have a department store in West Nashville?) during Christmas. It's our busiest season. I ran the gift wrapping booth. Had to work from 10 A.M. in the morning until 9:00 P.M. (while all my friends were out having a good time). And I didn't get paid, either. It's my contribution to the family, I guess. But it wasn't so bad, except that on Christmas Eve this drunk man came in and wanted me to wrap a present for his girlfriend. Drunk people scare me to death. I guess I'm just too young and inexperienced to deal with stuff like that. But I tried to stay calm and then you know what? When I was finished he gave me a fifty cent tip! That night after we closed the store, we had this big Christmas party for all the people that work for us and their families. We had eggnog and cakes, and we had a big Christmas tree that I got to help decorate. (My hands got all cut up from the angel hair.) It was fun for me, because Jewish people don't get to celebrate Christmas. I take that back. Some do, but they are not supposed to. To me Christmas is a lot of hard work, but it's okay because everyone acts real nice to everyone else.

I hope you managed to have a nice Christmas. I saw where Bob Hope was over there with all those movie stars entertaining the troops. I hope you got to see it. Did you receive the package? Did it get there in time for Xmas? Also did you get the picture? I hope you are not going to too much trouble on my account.

Well, it's almost a new year — 1954! I hope it will be a good one for you.

Fondly,
Lee Ann

Jan. 25, 1954
Kimpo, Korea

Dear Lee Ann,

I'm so glad you had fun in the Sunshine State. When my dad was in
the Marines, he was stationed in Pensacola and we lived there for a
while. Its hard to tear yourself away from all those wonderful
surroundings, ocean, sand, fruit groves, and good looking girls...
boys, in your case.

It's really nice about your work in the Sunday School. You're
making those college guys proud of you. When you start activities
like that, everyone will look up to you. I believe I was as thrilled as
you were about the play. It's my ambition to do just that. But only to
teach the youngsters. I was never brilliant, and I don't know if it's
possible for someone like me to be something. But if a person has it
in their soul, it is God's will and power to carry on in any event.
Right? I thought so. I guess, in your own way, you are kind of a
celebrity. You keep working on your ambitions, one never knows,
you might be world famous some day. Ha! Ha! But remember, you
can't be perfect. They just don't make them that way anymore.

I'm sorry you had to come up against that drunk. I'm sorry to
tell, but I know a lot about drunks — too much. Drinking ruins lives.
Lee Ann, I want to tell you about my sweet mother someday, if you
can spare a shoulder for my tears.

I received your wonderful package, and it did get here in time for
Christmas. I really needed the tee shirts (how did you know?) and
the magazines are wonderful. Thank you, thank you, thank you for
your thoughtfulness.

I got your picture, too. In fact I just got back from the painter's
place. I gave her strict instructions to do a great job on your picture.
Gosh! You're cute. I never realized I was writing anyone like you.
That picture in the paper didn't do you justice. She won't have any

trouble with it, I'm sure. There are only two doubts. Since I haven't been lucky enough to see you, I wouldn't know what color your eyes or hair are. I told her they were brown. I'm sorry if I was wrong. It will be all right, because I told her to get prepared to paint another one. I want to know what color your eyes, hair and eyebrows are. Also the color of the garment you were wearing. I promise to send the picture back to you. After she finishes it, I'll send both back at one time.

No, I don't think you are childish, just a wonderful little lady. And don't worry about my troubling myself over the picture. I love to help people.

Lee Ann, your letters have become a part of my life. Why? Because you are different. I've found many girls, but never one with Christianity as strong as yours. I hope with all my heart that you will find happiness throughout your entire life.

Forever a corresponding friend,

Tom

❖ ❖ ❖

March 1, '54
Nashville, Tenn.

Dear Tom,

I have been looking at your letter propped up on my desk for days now, and I feel bad every time I see it. I'm sorry that I have been so slow in writing you, but there never seems to be time. We had a big snow last week and everybody went crazy. You know how Nashville is. Everybody rushes out to the grocery store at the first snow flake, and they buy enough food for a month. It snowed about a foot — can you believe that? So, of course, we didn't have school. David came over, and we walked all the way over to my girlfriend's house. Her boyfriend was there, and we spent all afternoon playing charades, eating popcorn and dancing to La Vie en Rose. She's the one that got her nose fixed at Christmas break. Did I tell you about that? She had to go to Chicago to do it. Getting your nose fixed is an operation that breaks the bones in your nose and remolds it. It's called plastic surgery, but I don't think they really use plastic. Anyway, she came back all bandaged up and black and blue. But now she looks great. She was just a sweet-looking girl with a big nose when she left, and now she's gorgeous! It guess it was worth all the misery. Thank goodness, I won't have to do that. My nose is little, and it doesn't have a hump or anything.

Guess that's it for now.

Sincerely,
Lee Ann

❖   ❖   ❖

March 13, 1954
Nashville, Tenn.

Dear Tom,

I think yesterday was the worst day of my life. I know it was. And there is nobody I can talk to about it except you. I can't tell you exactly what happened, only that someone close to me, someone I love very much, told me something that has changed our relationship. This was someone I thought could do no wrong, someone perfect, someone I could depend on. My world was wonderful, and then this person told me their terrible, terrible secret and everything came tumbling down on me. Nothing will be the same between us now that I share the secret. I am very blue, and I can't even let on that I am blue. I know the world will go on. But I can never be a little girl anymore.

I know it is terrible for me to do this to you — not even tell you the whole story — but I swore not to and I never will.

I probably should tear up this letter, but somehow I need to send it. I know in my heart that you will understand. Thank you for being such a wonderful friend.

Sincerely,
Lee Ann

P.S. My hair and eyebrows are brown, but my eyes are green (but brown will do nicely) and my sweater was yellow, but any color is okay. I can't wait to see the picture.

L. A.

❖ ❖ ❖

March 24, '54
Kimpo, Korea

Dear Lee Ann,

This one may look horrible — due to an aching, throbbing head, it can't be helped.

I'll try to think straight. But nothing will keep me from answering your letter.

I am so proud you wrote me about your problem. It seems like all the time some buddy asks me a favor, advice, or puts his worries in my ears, because we are all lonely here. But when I write to a girl, I don't like to put my feelings of Korea within it. I'm just like all other humans, but I try to think out my problems myself. As I told you once before, I love to help my friends (and you especially). I stop whatever

I'm doing and listen. Using common sense, I put all effort to solve it, and they think there's nobody like Tom. Yes, I'm proud, or whatever you wish to say. Except conceit!! Lee Ann, I surely hope this isn't offending, but I despise a person with conceit. I only have credit to those who pay their debts. I am proud to know that you thought of me and wrote to me when you were in so much pain.

Say, thanks for the description. Your picture is on its way. It is very beautiful, just like you. You won't hurt my feelings if you want your own picture back. The reason I changed my mind about sending it with the painted one was I thought maybe you'd think I didn't want it. I do want it. I have it encased in a beautiful frame.

News is as rare around here as white mice, Lee Ann. They have been talking about moving out. Where? I don't know. But sometimes we have to work day and night. But when I get the time, I want to write you about my kid sister. She's about your age. I wish she was like you but she's not. My mother wrote that she was running around with a rough bunch, and I can't do anything about it, being over here. My mother has had so many hard times.

I'll close awaiting those three inch long words. I'll find me one, and we'll compete our vocabularies in a contest. How does that strike you?

Be as sweet as always and keep your chin up.

Your friend,
Tom

P.S. My APO number is 66 now. O.K.? Thanks. Tell all your family I said "Hello."

Good Night.
Tom

❖　❖　❖

April 30, 1954
Nashville, Tenn.

Dear Tom,

I am feeling much better than when I wrote to you last time. The wonderful picture arrived, and I thank you so very much. I showed it to everyone, and they are all impressed. You didn't tell me that it was going to be painted on silk!

Right now I am home sick in bed with the flu. There's an epidemic here in Nashville, and guess who was one of the first to get it. Yours truly. But I'm better. I've missed a week of school and I'm worried about that. I'm going to have soooo much to do. My boyfriend, David, has been bringing me my homework assignments, but I haven't felt much like doing them. David is really sweet. But sometimes he only thinks about himself. He can't help it, I know. And sometimes when I need to talk about something, he just clams up and won't say a thing, like he has put a wall up. But he is really cute and really smart, too. And a good athlete. I love him very much, but it is hard to be in love when you are only sixteen. It gets very complicated and tense sometimes. I am a very moral person, and so is he but sometimes I think we are going to end up going crazy. But then I think that after we're married, we'll have our whole lives together and that helps. Well, its time for my medicine — Yuk!

Tom, thank you again for the lovely picture. And by the way, I think you better send the other one back to me too.

Fondly,
Lee Ann

May 20, 1954
Kimpo, Korea

Dear Lee Ann,

I've been foolish. I should have known you were too sweet and modest to ask for the picture back. You were very nice and showed your raising. So, here it is. Since I have had it on my shelf, there have been many compliments passed. I was very proud to state, and brag about you being my pen pal, and from Nashville, too.

I'm at ease now to know your painted one arrived all right. I'm happy to know it was admired at your home.

Seems as though no letter can be perfect. I'm sorry you are one of the millions in the epidemic game.

I know what you mean when you say it's hard to be in love when you are sixteen. I too thought I was in love then, but sometimes we mistake other things for love. Right now I would go out with anybody. There aren't any girls over here except Korean ones, and I haven't gone out with any of them yet.

But the word is out that we might be rotated back to the States soon. It's too good to believe. Believe you me, I'm ready. I reckon by now you are probably getting ready for exams. That's the only thing I don't miss about school. I know you will do good. I'm sure, regardless of the feat, you'll be there before your competition. Good luck!

They have been working us hard lately, so I think I'll turn in.

Your friend,
Tom

June 15, 1954

"Hello."

"Hello. Is this Lori Sue?"

"No, it's Lee Ann. Who's this?"

"It's Tom, Lee Ann. Tom Holliway. I'm back. Here in Nashville. I...I know I wasn't supposed to call, but I just wanted to hear your voice. You...you sound so young."

"I don't know what to say. I'm so surprised. I know you must be very happy to be home."

"I just wanted to say thank you for writing to me. It made things so much easier."

"Oh...you're welcome. I was glad I could."

"Well...I guess I'll say good-bye now."

"Well...thank you...thank you for calling. Good luck."

Lee Ann slowly replaced the receiver.

"What wrong, honey? Who was that?" asked her mother walking into the room.

"Tom Holliway. He's back." Lee Ann glanced at her mother, saw her expression, then added, "Don't worry, he won't call back. I wasn't very nice to him. I cut him short."

Lee Ann put down the newspaper and pushed her chair away from the table. All these years, she thought, he lived right here in Nashville. I could have passed him on the street. I didn't even know what he looked like. She gathered up the dishes and placed them in the kitchen sink.

I wonder if he ever thought about me. Lord knows, living here in Nashville, he would have seen things in the newspaper. There was almost half a page of pictures from my wedding, then all the stuff that I did in the community. My life's been an open book, and I bet he read it.

And what do I know of him? He was a preacher. That makes sense. I wonder if he had a following? Was he able to help people? Did his wife love him? Was he happy? Was he able to forgive me?

Lee Ann took a scissors out of the kitchen drawer, walked over to the breakfast room table and carefully clipped the obituary from the newspaper.

JIMMY GREY

❦ 1980 ❧

Why did I do this to myself? Lee Ann thought, as she slowed her car to a stop at the red light on Deaderick Street. I could have refused and not put myself through all this aggravation. Could've, but I didn't. She reached up and tilted the rearview mirror toward herself. She smiled a half smile at her reflection. You just couldn't resist seeing him again, could you, Lee Ann? She scanned her face, checking her makeup. Not bad for forty-three, she thought. The mid-morning traffic began to ease forward. Lee Ann readjusted the mirror and continued on down the street until she reached the parking garage of the United National Bank. Before leaving the car, she hesitated, snapped open her purse and removed a small packet of note cards, which she studied briefly. Replacing the cards, she opened her compact for one last look. A wave of adrenaline coursed through her as finally she reached for the handle of the car door. It's like taking the summer's first plunge into a still-cold pool, she thought — half of you wants to and the other half doesn't.

The bank lobby reverberated with hushed-edged voices. The clicking of her heels on the marble floor echoed against the metal and glass of the ultra-modern building. This is not my taste, she thought, and shuddered at its iciness. There was something about the bank itself that troubled her, something she knew was there but couldn't quite fathom. The uniformed attendant motioned her into a waiting car in the bank of elevators. The elevator was already crowded with young men in seemingly identical business suits and shimmery-silk clad young women. Her nostrils, filling with the blended aromas of aftershave and perfume, heightened her awareness of the unfamiliar.

It was only when she emerged from the elevator on the executive floor that she began to feel at home. The setting resembled the elegant foyer of a southern mansion. Taylor Jackson outdid himself on this one, she thought, as she admired the handiwork of the outstanding Nashville architect. A gilt-framed notice board announced, 'Dining Room closed today. Children's Trauma Center Luncheon 12:30.' Just reading the sign made Lee Ann feel queasy.

Well, there's no turning back now, she said to herself, as she watched the pretty receptionist get up from behind the Queen Anne desk and come toward her.

"Mrs. Marlowe, so nice to see you," she purred.

Lee Ann had to repress the giggle building inside her as the image of her old family maid, Hattie Mae, emerged saying, "Lawd, I sure wishd I had me a spoon to scoop up all that powdered sugar falling off that chile."

"Mr. Grey wanted me to show you right in, but a bank emergency has come up and he's not able to get out of his meeting just yet, so he asked me to take you to the private reception room until he's free. This way, please," she said, as she started down the long oak paneled corridor. "Mr. Grey is really so sorry. I hope this won't inconvenience you." She ushered Lee Ann into a small sitting room. "May I bring you a cup of coffee?"

Lee Ann nodded and watched as the silk dress swished its retreat down the hall. She walked over to a mahogany credenza, picked up a magazine, and sat down in the powder blue wing chair facing the door. She thumbed through the magazine, but her thoughts were on Jimmy Grey. Jimmy Grey. If he only knew...if he had any idea who I really was, how I've watched him...all these years. She felt a hot flush rising up from her neck flooding her cheeks. Headlines...all those headlines. I devoured them. *Jimmy Grey, Tennessee Athlete of the Year — Jimmy Grey Chooses Football — Jimmy Grey Wins Scholarship to U. of Michigan — Jimmy Grey, Rose Bowl Hero — Jimmy Grey Drafted by the Dallas Cowboys — Jimmy Grey, Brilliant Career Ended by Injury.* For twenty-five years...twenty-five years, I have stalked him. That's what I've done...and he never knew it. I never told...never told anyone, not David, not anyone.

They had met, of course. One couldn't live in Nashville and run around in the circles they did and not meet now and again. After all, he was a prominent banker and she was a community leader, the wife of a respected businessman. They had been introduced at the Swan Ball, and he had even been in her home once...at the party for the new Chancellor of Vanderbilt. But this would be different. It would just be...the two of them.

"Here we are," said the receptionist, as she placed a silver tea service on the butler's table. "The cook didn't have any cookies today, so I brought you some beaten biscuits. I hope you don't mind."

"Not at all. You really shouldn't have gone to so much trouble."

"Happy to do it. If you need anything, anything at all, just dial 23," she said, motioning to the phone on the credenza, and gently closed the door as she left the room.

Lee Ann poured herself a cup of steaming black coffee. She picked up the cup and saucer. The cup rattled against the saucer. Calm down, silly! She took a deep breath and, cup in hand, walked over to a tall window and looked out. Beyond the ugly, splayed rooftops, she caught a glimpse of the Cumberland River and a patch of green grass on the riverbank.

The memory of the high school cafeteria came back with sudden clarity. That was it, she thought, the first time I met Jimmy Grey. It was in that cafeteria...after a game. I must have been...fifteen. Lee Ann tried to imagine herself then. The blue cheerleading skirt, the gray sweater with the big blue W, her trademark long brown ponytail. And Jimmy Grey. He was so good-looking...the basketball star from East High. A sock hop after the game.

"Would you like to dance?" he had asked.

Me! He was asking me to dance. Of all the girls...he had chosen me! Lee Ann felt a little shiver slide down her back as the touch of Jimmy Grey's hand penetrated her consciousness. It had been so strong, so self-assured. Her hand had felt so small, secure in his. There had been something immediate...electric...between them. Lee Ann tried to remember the music. It was slow, dreamy.

"What's your name?" he had asked.

"Lee Ann," she had said, "Lee Ann Blumberg."

He had stared at her, his blue-gray eyes searching her face. She had felt suddenly exposed, revealed. Then David cut in. David! He had been so jealous!

"Can I have my girl back?" he said, as he pulled her away.

"Thanks. Thanks for the dance, Lee Ann."

As she and David walked away, she could feel Jimmy Grey's eyes following her. Nothing would...could...come of it. He was gentile and she was Jewish. She didn't date gentile boys. But she had daydreamed about Jimmy Grey in the week that followed...until...until everything turned upside down.

How well she remembered that day. The day it happened. It had begun innocently enough. David had driven her home after school. Hattie Mae was in the kitchen listening to her 'stories' on the radio.

"Hi, Hattie Mae. What's up? Where's Mama?"

Hattie Mae turned the volume down on 'Stella Dallas.'

"Nothin' much," she said. "Mizris Rosalyn took Miz Lori Sue to get her braces put on."

Lee Ann smiled. "That'll be a sight. There'll be some whining going on around here tonight. Got anything good in the icebox?"

She draped David's letter jacket on the back of a kitchen chair and opened the refrigerator.

"You wouldn't believe this day, Hattie Mae! The whole school was buzzing about the ball game last night. Nobody can believe we're going to the State Championship. I bet we win, too. No one's going to get a lick of work done."

"Yo flyin' mighty high, Miz Lee Ann."

"Oh. Hattie Mae, you're such a party-pooper."

Lee Ann spread some peanut butter on a slice of bread and headed for the den.

"Miz Lee Ann, I clean forgot! Mr. George called. He wants yo to call him the minute yo gets home."

"Daddy? Did he say what he wanted?"

"No'm, but yo best call him," said Hattie Mae, handing Lee Ann the telephone.

Lee Ann dialed the store.

"Claudine? Hi, this is Lee Ann. My daddy around?"

"Hold on, Lee Ann. I think he just came in."

In a few seconds, George Blumberg's voice came on the line.

"Lee Ann? You home?"

Something in his tone…"Yes, Daddy I just walked in. Is something wrong?"

"No, just stay there. I want to talk to you. I'll be there in twenty minutes."

The phone clicked and he was gone.

"What's the matter, honey?"

"Oh, I don't know. Daddy just sounded…funny. Where's Mama?"

"She dun took Miz…"

"The braces. I forgot. Hattie Mae, you don't think something bad could have happened?"

"Lawd, honey, what yo sayin.' Yo lettin' that imagination run away wid yo agin."

"Guess so."

"Why don't yo finish yo sammich? Yo wanna glass of milk?"

Lee Ann shook her head and put the rest of the peanut butter sandwich in the trash.

"I'll be back in my room," she said, as she gathered up her schoolbooks and headed down the hall to her bedroom.

She always headed to her room when things went the wrong way. Why can't things just be nice and normal? Why do things always have to pop up and disrupt everything? Why couldn't Daddy have said what he wanted over the phone?

Lee Ann liked her room, her private territory, even if the flowery fabric for the bedspreads and curtains had been selected by that weird decorator her mother used. But today it offered little comfort. She sat at her desk and opened the World History text to the assigned chapter. "Can't concentrate," she said and slammed the book shut.

She went across the hall to the den and flipped on the television set. Mr. Wizard was conducting an experiment with electricity, using a pan of water and a magnet. She flipped the channels, but all she got was snow. The reception here stinks, she thought.

The telephone rang and she ran to answer it.

"Oh, Grandma Dora, how are you feeling? No, Mama's not at home. I'll tell her you called. Oh yes, I know I haven't seen you all week. But you know how it is with school and all. I'll see you Friday night and I'll tell Mama you called. Bye."

She replaced the receiver. George Blumberg was standing in the doorway. One look at her father and she knew she had been right. Something was very wrong. If there was one special quality about George Blumberg, it was the warmth he exuded. The merry sparkle in his eyes, his rosy smile…he seemed to glow. But not today. He looked vague, unfocused, his lips drawn across his teeth, his skin blanched. Lee Ann ran over to him for a hug but he stepped back.

"Daddy?!"

Lee Ann stared at this unknown face. This was her father, her soul mate, the one person in the world with whom she felt completely at ease, the defender of her choices, the champion of all her efforts. For Lee Ann he had always been the embodiment of manhood — physically strong, morally correct, self-made, consistent. Suddenly she felt estranged, tentative.

"Get your coat, honey. Let's go for a ride."

Lee Ann followed him down the hall and back through the kitchen, picking up her jacket on the way. Hattie Mae watched the procession in uncharacteristic silence.

Once in the car, Lee Ann waited for her father to speak. She burned with questions. George didn't look at her. He appeared to be concentrating on his driving, but Belle Meade Boulevard was practically deserted. Silence filled the space between them. Lee Ann, not wanting to stare at him, tried to focus on the elegant homes that lined the boulevard. She knew who lived in most of them but had never been inside any. The only Jews she knew that had were David and his family.

George drove through the massive stone gates that marked the entrance to Percy Warner Park. The road wound upward into the forest, and only when the car reached the parking niche high above the entrance did he reach over and switch off the motor.

He sank back against the leather seat. His hand began massaging the old war wound in his thigh. Lee Ann tensed, her senses finely tuned.

"Lee Ann," he broke the silence. "...why did you call Jimmy Grey?"

"Jimmy Grey?" Lee Ann blushed. "The basketball player?" Jimmy Grey! That was the last thing she expected to come out of her father's mouth.

"Daddy," she said recovering, "what's going on? You didn't drag me out here and scare me half to death just because I called a boy."

"You met him?"

"Who?"

"Jimmy Grey!"

"After the game last week. But nothing happened. I just danced with him for a few minutes. I can dance with gentile boys, can't I? There's nothing wrong with that."

"What did he say to you?"

"Nothing!"

Once again she felt the color rise on her face as she recalled the voice and touch of Jimmy Grey.

"Daddy, he was very nice, very good-looking...and a great basketball player. I was flattered that he asked me to dance. That's all."

Her right thumb began to feel numb, a headache starting.

"How...how did you know?"

She had called Jimmy Grey.

"Hello," a woman's voice answered.

"May I speak to Jimmy, please?"

"He's not here right now, honey. Can I give him a message?"

"Well, I...I guess so. This is Lee Ann Blumberg. I'm a cheerleader at West, and I watched him play the other night and just wanted to tell him how good I thought he was."

"What did you say your name was?"

"Lee Ann. Lee Ann Blumberg. Could you ask Jimmy to phone me please? My number is..."

The phone clicked off.

"It was nothing, Daddy. Nothing. Stupid, just stupid. I've never done anything like that before. You know me. I'm really shy about stuff like that. I don't know what made me do it."

Lee Ann waited for a reaction, a response, but none came.

"I can't explain it. All the girls have crushes on him. I did call him, but he wasn't even there." Then she smiled and shook her head. "I probably would have hung up when he got on the phone. I wouldn't have known what to say."

She stopped and searched her father's face, trying to make some sense out of all of this. He didn't seem to be hearing anything she was saying.

"Look, Daddy, I'm sorry I called him, but I only talked to his mother." Lee Ann hesitated a moment. "You know, I hadn't thought about it 'til now, but his mother had been so friendly right up until the time I left my name. I thought we got disconnected...but she hung up on me! Didn't she? Didn't she, Daddy? Why? What is it? Does she have something against the Blumbergs? Is she anti-Semitic? Do you know her?"

Lee Ann took a sip of the now cold coffee and bit into the beaten biscuit. Yuk, tasteless, she thought, I wonder why they make such a big deal over these things. She walked back to the blue chair and looked down at her watch. Almost 12:00.

She would never forget that day, the day her father took her to Percy Warner Park. At first she had thought it was a Jewish-gentile thing. But when her father leaned his head against the steering wheel and began to sob, she knew there was more. She had never seen him cry, not even when Papa Ben died.

She put her hand on his arm and heard him say, "Don't see him again, Lee Ann. Promise me!"

"You know I won't, Daddy. But I don't understand."

Her father raised his head and looked at her, his face stained and mottled.

"You don't need to, Lee Ann. Just don't have anything to do with him, and it will be all right."

"You're wrong, Daddy. You are hiding something from me, and it's like a big wall between us."

George covered his face with his hands and rubbed the tips of his fingers across his eyes, then let them drop to his lap.

"This is the last thing I wanted to happen. I never wanted to involve you or your mother. I thought I could protect you. I love you, Lee Ann. More than anything in the world. Damn it, I shouldn't have let this happen. I should have been able to protect you."

"Protect me from what?"

"Things happen. They happen."

He buried his face in his hands. Lee Ann heard his muffled voice saying, "This is a punishment, a punishment. I can't take a chance. Can't." He looked up, his eyes filled with tears.

"Daddy, don't. I love you. You know that."

"Lee Ann, honey, I...I...," George thumped the steering wheel hard with his fist.

"Lee Ann, Jimmy Grey..." George took a deep breath and expelled it slowly. "Jimmy Grey is my son."

Lee Ann shook her head in disbelief.

"That can't be!"

She felt her lips start to tingle and the numbness in her thumb spread across her hand.

"Lee Ann, honey, listen. It happened a long time ago. I was only twenty-one years old! I was working for Papa Ben, at his store on Cedar Street, and so was she...Darlene."

Entrance to Percy Warner Park

"Don't say her name. Don't say any more."

Lee Ann put her hands over her ears.

"Lee Ann, you have to hear me out." George's voice was raspy.

She took her hands away.

He softened his voice and continued. "She was so pretty, so very pretty...and sweet. I was drawn to her like a magnet. We were together every day, working. And when we weren't, she was on my mind."

George stroked the wheel as he spoke.

"I was smitten. And she felt the same way about me."

George closed his eyes for a moment.

"But she was a *shiksa* and Church of Christ. We both knew our feelings for each other were forbidden. We were so innocent and so stupid! Anyway, one day she told me she thought she was pregnant and, as it turned out, she was!"

"Maybe it wasn't yours. Maybe it was somebody else's. It could have been somebody else's."

"Honey, I knew it was mine. I never had any doubt. Darlene was very religious and, in spite of what happened, very moral."

He gripped the steering wheel.

"And there was no question of terminating the pregnancy. Darlene was Church of Christ, and to them abortion is a greater sin than having a child out of wedlock."

Abortion! Out of wedlock! Lee Ann fought against the strange words. She struggled to force out the images. Her father younger, the pretty blond Darlene. Where? In a car? In the park? How could he have a life she knew nothing about? She felt a squeezing pressure in her head, her brain contracting. She reached for the door handle.

George put his hand on her arm and held her.

"Wait, Lee Ann, listen to me. It all happened a long time ago, before I met Mama. I was very young and..."

"No, no!"

Pulling away, she opened the door and bolted from the car. She ran across the road and onto a bridle path winding upward through the thicket. Half blinded by tears, she plunged deeper and deeper into the woods. Overhanging trees and ground brush grabbed at her clothing and pulled at her hair. In the distance, she could hear her father's voice calling to her.

A gnarled sycamore root ran across the horse-worn path. The toe of Lee Ann's saddle oxford got caught in the pocket between the root and the path. She plunged face forward into the leaves and brush, her twisted foot still trapped in the root.

When George finally reached her, she was sitting up holding her ankle. He dropped down on his knees beside her.

"What happened? Are you all right? Let me see?"

He removed her sock and massaged the ankle. Then he dabbed at the scratches on her face with his handkerchief, using her own tears to clean them. They sat side by side on the winter-hardened ground. The smell of pine and dead wood began to intensify as the sun sank behind the hill and the air chilled. Rain, tapping the leaves that sheltered them, was the only sound.

Her ankle ached and the pain in her head sharpened.

"What did you do?" she blurted.

"Honey, I didn't know what to do. It made me sick, physically sick. I couldn't think, couldn't work. Some of the guys in my crowd had a fishing camp up on the Tennessee River. Just a hut, really. I went up there. Stayed a week. Half the time I slept, and the other half I racked my brain trying to find a way out. In the end I knew what I had to do."

Lee Ann turned toward him. In the half-light, his features blurred.

"I came back and told Papa Ben. It was the hardest thing I ever had to do. Dad thought I hung the moon, that I could do no wrong. He lived by a strict code of right and wrong. He saw immorality as a weakness. I knew I was going to break his heart."

George groped on the ground for his handkerchief. He mopped at the tears streaming down his face. Lee Ann watched him reliving the experience, the fragments cutting away at him.

"He was so kind, so incredibly kind. He hugged me...hugged me. And me twice as big as he was."

George stopped; his head bent forward, eyes down.

"He let me know that he disapproved." Then he looked at Lee Ann. "No, it was stronger than that. He said it in Yiddish."

Lee Ann heard him whisper the unfamiliar Yiddish words.

"*Brawch tzoo mihr. Aveira...aveira.* A curse to me. A sin...a sin."

George cleared his throat and swallowed hard.

"He let me know in no uncertain terms that what had happened was abhorrent. But then he said he understood and that we had to go forward, make a plan for Darlene...and the baby. He called Darlene in, and the three of us sat in his little office in the back of the store. Darlene would stop working. Dad would put a thousand dollars in a special bank account in her name, and I would add a part of my paycheck each week."

George shifted his weight and looked at Lee Ann, his eyes not quite meeting hers.

"Lee Ann, a thousand dollars was a fortune in those days,

especially for my father. The only time I ever heard from her was the day after the baby was born. She called to tell me it was a boy and that he was healthy. Later, when I had my own business, I arranged for an automatic transfer each month. It was a terrible mistake, but I wanted it to be over. I tried to get it out of my mind, like some bad dream. Then, after all those years, the publicity started in the newspaper, and last month I saw his picture. It tore me to bits. I was so proud of him...so disgusted with myself."

Lee Ann picked up a stick and began scratching in the dirt.

"I bet she hated you."

Silence.

She threw the stick away and looked at her father.

"Daddy, how could...how could you walk away, pretend it didn't happen? It was a child, a living, breathing child. Your son! My....." The word stuck in her throat.

"Oh, my God! Oh, God! I danced with him."

Lee Ann buried her head between her drawn-up knees.

"Lee Ann, don't!"

She straightened and stared at him through the darkness.

"How does Mama feel about this?"

George didn't answer.

"Mama does...she does know about this, doesn't she?"

"She doesn't know, nobody knew, except Papa Ben and Darlene...and now, you. I don't think the boy knows. Darlene married before he was born. A decent guy, I think. I don't think she would tell the boy."

"Daddy, how can you keep something like this from Mama? It's not right...not fair."

George got to his knees.

"I always intended to tell her. But she got pregnant with you so soon, and then...there never was a good time. I just couldn't dredge it up again."

George hoisted himself up and extended his hand to Lee Ann.

"We'd better get back. I have to close the store. You ride with me?"

Lee Ann nodded.

Father and daughter slowly made their way down the dark, steep path, leaning against each other for support. Seated in the car, Lee Ann asked, "How are we going to explain this to Mama? You know Hattie Mae's already said something, and look what a mess I am."

"We'll have to think of something, some reason."

"Daddy, I can't lie to Mama. I won't tell her, but I won't lie either."

By the time they reached the store, Lee Ann's headache had subsided to a dull throb. George pulled into his parking space and cut off the motor. He turned and looked at her.

"It will be all right, Daddy. It'll be all right."

She had meant it to be encouraging, but her voice sounded forced and flat.

She watched her father get out of the car and walk away limping slightly. Just before he rounded the corner of the building, he turned and waved. At that moment she realized that they would never speak of this again.

"Mrs. Marlowe, Mr. Grey can see you now. Mrs. Marlowe?"

"Oh!" said Lee Ann, jolted back to reality.

"I'm sorry. I didn't mean to startle you." Then, extending her arm in the direction of the door, she said, "This way, please."

Lee Ann followed the young woman down the corridor to the oversized oak paneled door at the end. The brass lettering on the door said: Executive Vice-President. The receptionist tapped on the door, then opened it.

"Mrs. Marlowe is here, Mr. Grey."

Jimmy Grey stood up and went to greet the tall, brunette woman who entered his office. I didn't remember her being so attractive, he thought, taking in the green eyes and slim figure beneath the salmon pink suit. She's some classy lady. Cool it, Jimmy, she's off limits…way off limits.

"Mr. Grey, how nice to see you again," she said extending her hand.

"Please, it's Jimmy," he said as he clasped it.

"Only if you call me Lee Ann."

Oh, no, she thought, as a familiar tinge ran through her fingers.

"Please have a seat, Lee Ann. I'm sorry I kept you waiting. I had been looking forward to having some time to speak with you about the Trauma Center before the luncheon."

As he spoke, Lee Ann allowed herself to look at the man who seated himself across from her. He had her father's broad shoulders and the look of an athlete. Seeing those familiar eyes and smile superimposed on a strange face caused her pulse to quicken.

"When I assumed the presidency of the Children's Trauma Center," Jimmy was saying, "I heard so much about all the good work you had done there. Everyone from the medical staff to the porters sang your praises. You have created something exceptional. But that's what today is all about, isn't it? Paying tribute to your efforts."

Lee Ann interrupted. "Please, I didn't do it alone. It was the combined talents of a great many people."

Jimmy smiled. "Of course." He stretched his long legs out. "We're expecting a great turnout today. A real cross-section of the community. The governor is…"

"Sending his representative?"

Jimmy laughed. "You've done this kind of thing before."

"Lot of times. Only I've never been on the receiving end before. I find it very uncomfortable. But I guess we have to have events like this to generate interest in the Center. Tell me, Jimmy, how did you get involved with all of this?"

"Last year my youngest boy, Gary, was in a pretty bad accident. Riding a bicycle, no helmet. We almost lost him. If it hadn't been for the Trauma Center, we probably would have."

"How is he now?"

"Almost a hundred percent."

This is my nephew we're talking about! And I don't even know him! I will never know him. This man is my brother, there is part of me in him and part of him in me...and we are strangers!

She couldn't bring herself to look directly at Jimmy Grey. A delicate knock on the door broke the tension.

"Excuse me, Mr. Grey," the receptionist said, opening the door, the photographer is here from the newspaper. He wants a picture of you and Mrs. Marlowe for tomorrow's edition."

While the photographer was positioning them, standing side by side holding a banner emblazoned with the logo of the Trauma Center, the reality that a picture of herself with Jimmy Grey would appear in the morning paper jarred Lee Ann. She envisioned her father sitting down at a booth at the Koffee Kup, unfolding the newspaper, and seeing the picture of his two children. Her head was swimming. She felt flushed and out of control.

"Smile," said the photographer.

Jimmy looked at his watch. "It's time for lunch. We'd better join the others. We'll have to get together another time and talk about the Center."

They reached the Executive Dining Room, which was rapidly filling up with people. Black men in tuxedo pants and starched white jackets skillfully wove their way among the guests, offering petite cheese biscuits, mushrooms with bread stuffing, boiled shrimp daintily skewered on colorful toothpicks, and tinkling crystal glasses filled with white wine.

"Lee Ann, do you know Mayor Collins?" Jimmy asked, as they

greeted the small, rotund man whose firm grip on city politics had endured for almost two decades.

"Of course, how are you, Dan?" responded Lee Ann. "I have been meaning to call to congratulate you on your handling of that school situation last week. It was a stroke of genius, and with this whole busing mess heating up again."

Jimmy excused himself. "Be back in a minute. Enjoy yourselves."

Lee Ann chattered on with the mayor, looking over his shoulder from time to time at Jimmy Grey and the ease with which he worked the crowd. He's a people person, she thought, didn't get that from Daddy.

The mayor, who rarely missed anything, remarked: "The Bank sure got lucky when they got Jimmy Grey. You know the old Nashville saying, Lee Ann, old racehorses get put out to pasture, and old athletes go to work for the bank. Take that one, for example," he said, as a tall, jovial-faced man approached with Jimmy in tow. "Jesse Waverly's claim to fame is that he once played defense for the Pittsburgh Steelers, and that he knows the life story and telephone number of everybody in Nashville."

"Well, if it ain't two of my all time favorite people," said Jesse, as he swung a massive arm around the diminutive mayor. Addressing himself to Jimmy, Jesse continued: "The mayor here is one helluva fella, and I've known Miss Lee Ann Blumberg, now Mrs. Marlowe, since we were in the fourth grade at Ransom School."

Lee Ann cringed at the childhood reference and the phony familiarity. She looked up to see how all this pseudo-friendliness registered with Jimmy and caught a puzzled expression on his face.

"Where's the Mister?" Jesse queried. "Thought he'd be here on your big day."

"David? Unfortunately he threw his back out on the tennis court last weekend. The doctor threatened him with surgery if he didn't stay in bed. So that's where he is, mad as a wet hen, too."

The group gravitated toward the enormous dining room table covered in white linen and adorned with Tiffany and Wedgewood. Once everyone was seated, the room quieted for the clergyman's invocation. His "in Jesus' name we pray" not only signaled the waiters to enter with their steaming trays, but it goaded Lee Ann into turning to Jimmy, who was seated to her left, and saying, "I wish you could do something about that."

"About what?"

"Oh, goodness, I get so exasperated. Can you imagine what it's like to be Jewish and have to listen to "in Jesus' name we pray" before every luncheon or dinner you go to? I'm not all that religious, but it really gets to me."

"I never thought about it, Lee Ann. Seems so…natural to me. I'd be glad to see what I can do."

"Thank you. I should have done it myself a long time ago, but I just never got up the gumption. Guess I was afraid it might start a row, and I hate rows."

He's not even Jewish, she thought.

Jimmy shifted his chair until he was almost facing Lee Ann. He seemed hesistant, then asked, "Did Jesse say your name was Blumberg?"

The water in Lee Ann's upraised glass sloshed over her hand.

"Darn it!"

She mopped up the spill with her napkin. He couldn't know, surely. "It used to be," she replied.

"Mr. Ben Blumberg's granddaughter?"

Lee Ann stared at Jimmy. "Yes."

"Well, how about that!" Jimmy said with a big grin. "Mr. Ben was one of the finest men I ever knew."

"You…you knew Papa Ben?"

"Sure did, real well, he and my mother were good friends. She worked for him before I was born. So he kind of took me under his wing."

Jimmy paused. "I owe a lot to Mr. Ben. You know, Lee Ann, I probably wouldn't have gotten this far if it hadn't been for him. He never missed a birthday, always was my number one fan. He just kept encouraging me in everything I did. I think he even helped my folks out during hard times. He never told you about me? Lord, he talked about you all the time."

Lee Ann felt the room closing in as the waiter removed her plate. She tried to think of an excuse to get up...to leave...but the chairman of the luncheon had already begun to make his presentation.

Oh, Papa Ben. Papa Ben.

"You know," Jimmy whispered, "I even went to his funeral...at the synagogue. It was the first time I had been in a Jewish synagogue. I was scared silly. Stood way in the back. And I cried, couldn't help it. You would have thought he was my own grandfather."

Polite applause rippled through the crowd.

"You're not going to believe this, but I danced with you once. At a high school party. I was shocked out of my mind when you said your name was Lee Ann Blumberg. I never told Mr. Ben about it. Don't think he'd have been too thrilled, his granddaughter dancing with the likes of me," Jimmy grinned. "I can't believe that, after all these years, we're actually sitting here together."

The stuffed mushrooms began tumbling around in Lee Ann's stomach. Hot tears stood just behind her eyes. She heard her name and realized that she was being introduced. Jimmy got up to help her out of her chair. He plucked a rose from a vase on the table and handed it to Lee Ann. Then, linking her arm in his, he escorted her to the podium.

SYLVIA

❦ 1991 ❧

"**I** remember the night Sylvia was born, clear as when it happened. Maybe I can't remember what happened yesterday, but I sure can remember that night." Selma sat in her wheelchair beside her cousin Rosalyn and watched her light the *Yartzeit* candle and place it on the tray of the silver service. "I was only eleven years old. It must have been...What? Let's see. I'm eighty-two. So it was seventy-one years ago. Can you believe that, Rosalyn? 1920! You and I were both there that night Sylvia was born. And here we are, still here, and Sylvia long dead."

"It was a terrible night in the dead of winter. There was an ice storm, one of those terrible Nashville ice storms that always precede a snowfall. We got a call from Aunt Dora about eight in the evening, a desperate, screaming call. Mama spun into action. 'Bernie,' she called to Papa, 'go warm up the car. Dora's baby is coming and Jake's gone out. We need to get over there right away.' She turned to my oldest brother, Bennie, and said, 'Aunt Dora's number is on the pad by the phone. Get the others to bed. I don't know when we'll be back.' Then she looked at me. 'Selma, get your warm coat and gloves, you're coming with us.' I couldn't believe Mama had chosen me to go with them. I felt so important and a little frightened.

Like I said, it was a terrible night. The road was already a sheet of solid ice. It took us thirty minutes to get to your house, Rosalyn, and it was only a mile away. Just getting from the car to the front door was a peril. In our hurry to get to Aunt Dora, we had forgotten our boots, and our hard-soled shoes slid on the ice.

The house was dark when we finally made it to the front porch. The electrical wires had snapped under the weight of the ice, and the whole neighborhood had been plunged into darkness.

'Oh, My God! I hope the phone still works,' said Mama. 'I hope Dora got through to Doctor Rosenberg!'

'For God's Sake, why did Jake go out on a night like this?' asked Papa, as we rapped on the door.

'I don't know, Dora said something about a burst pipe in one of his rentals. He couldn't know she would go into labor so soon.'

We saw a movement behind the lace curtain that covered the glass panel in the front door. We could barely make out the small face, but it was you, Rosalyn, peeping out through the pushed aside curtain. We sensed more than saw you in the darkness.

'Rosalyn, Honey, open the door for Aunt Minnie,' Mama called out.

We heard you fiddling with the lock.

'Just turn it. Turn it towards Mr. Adams' house, sugar,' Mama pleaded.

We heard the lock fall and rushed inside, Mama calling out orders as she ran back to Aunt Dora's bedroom. 'Bernie, find some candles. They are in one of the kitchen drawers. Selma, you are in charge of Rosalyn. Try to get her to bed.'

I took your hand and we groped our way down the hall to your bedroom. You already had on your nightgown.

I turned back the covers on the bed. I could hear Aunt Dora moaning in the next room. I knew you were terrified. You were only four years old. You couldn't understand what was happening. I wasn't really sure myself. It was impossible to read to you because of the dark, even after Papa brought us in a candle. So I started singing. It seemed like we sang every song we knew. You were already fading out when I heard Papa letting Dr. Rosenberg in. I began to sing more softly, humming really, and in a little while you closed your eyes and your little chest rose and fell in the sleep rhythm. I loosened your fingers from around my hand and slowly got up from the bed, tucking the cover around you.

Taking the candle with me, I walked out into the hall. I could hear the voices coming from the kitchen and Aunt Dora screaming.

'Damn you, Jake. Damn you. How could you do this to me!'

The kitchen had been transformed into a birthing room. Candles had been placed all around. Everything was shadowy and golden. The flickering of the candles made it dreamlike. Aunt Dora lay on the white enamel kitchen table, with a bed pillow under her head and a white sheet over her body. Her knees were sticking out from underneath and looked as white as the sheet. Mama was putting warm compresses on her forehead and whispering softly to her. Doctor Rosenberg was at the foot of the table, his hands pressing on her mountainous abdomen.

I could see Aunt Dora's body begin to tense up.

'Now, Dora. Push, push!'

My mama grimaced in pain as Aunt Dora clutched her arm.

'Oh, God,' Aunt Dora screamed. 'Kill me, kill me, I want to die.'

That's what she said, Rosalyn. Kill me. I want to die. It scared me to death.

'I can see the head, Dora. Push, push!' yelled Dr. Rosenberg. 'We're almost there!'

I hadn't even heard him come in, but suddenly your daddy, Uncle Jake, was in the room. He ran over to Aunt Dora, grabbed her hand and reached down to kiss her. She slapped him away. She treated Uncle Jake like that, you know, wouldn't let him get close to her.

Aunt Dora screamed again and Dr. Rosenberg lifted the baby, little Sylvia, out.

After Mama had washed Sylvia, she handed her to Uncle Jake.

'Dora, my precious,' he said. 'We have another baby girl. A healthy baby girl. Look, *Bubele*, a *sheina meidl*. Our little Sylvia.'

'The baby? No, no, too tired. Go away, Jake. Leave me alone. Go away with all your happiness.'

Rosalyn stepped behind Selma's chair and wheeled her into the kitchen. She had heard this story before, many times. Its familiarity was comforting. Twice a year, Rosalyn and her daughter, Lee Ann, drove to Memphis to pick up Selma at the Jewish Home for the Aged and brought her to Nashville for a visit. She came for the High Holy Days, which always coincided with Sylvia's *yartzeit*, and she came again at Passover.

Rosalyn had been worried about putting Selma in the home, but after Selma had broken her hip for the second time, there seem to be no choice. The decision had fallen on her shoulders since Selma had never had any children of her own and Rosalyn was her nearest living relative. Selma hadn't complained and seemed comfortable there. Still, Rosalyn knew that the two visits to Nashville were very important to Selma.

And Selma was important to Rosalyn, too. She was Rosalyn's last link to her past, the only one left alive who knew, who understood.

She pushed Selma up to the dinette table and asked, "You want coffee or tea?"

"Just hot water and lemon, thanks."

Rosalyn walked over to the sink and filled the kettle. There were no windows in the kitchen and Rosalyn regretted that. It was the only thing she disliked about the Windsor Towers. At first, she had rejected the idea of living in a high-rise. She didn't want to give up her privacy and her garden. Five years had passed since she had made the move, and she felt the trade off had been worth it. She was glad to be relieved of the garden and was content with her houseplants. The companionship of the other Jewish women in the building relieved the loneliness she had felt when her husband, George, had died.

"Your mother wasn't a bad person," Selma said as Rosalyn placed the cup in front of her. "I really liked Aunt Dora, in spite of everything. She was such a beautiful woman. Even at her worst times, she looked good. And she could do anything she set her mind to. She made beautiful clothes and was a wonderful cook. It was just the sickness that robbed her. I could forgive her everything... everything except Sylvia."

Rosalyn cut two slices of sponge cake and spooned cut up strawberries over each piece, letting the juice saturate them. She served Selma and then herself.

"The strange thing was that Sylvia adored our mother," Rosalyn said. "She followed her around like a puppy dog, hung on her every word. I was the rebel. I'd talk back to Mama. But Sylvia wouldn't. She let Mama dominate her. I guess they would call it a form of child abuse today. Mama didn't hit her, but she broke her spirit just the same."

"You know, the two sisters, our mothers, had a hard childhood. Their own mother died so young, just after they arrived in this country. Their tata couldn't take care of them and put them in the Jewish Children's Orphanage in Cincinnati for a while. That must have been very difficult. I don't know whether that's what unbalanced Aunt Dora, or if she would have been that way regardless. The orphanage didn't seem to have an ill effect on my mother, at least not any long term effect."

"Aunt Minnie? Your mother was a rock and an angel, so solid and dependable and kind-hearted. I've never known anyone as grounded as she was. Sylvia and I always knew we could go to Aunt Minnie with our problems. We loved being at your house. There was so much happiness there. Aunt Minnie had all those children, but she always made the two of us feel so welcome. She moved us in every time Mama had to go to the sanatorium. It seems like I spent most of my childhood at your house."

Rosalyn took a sip of her tea. "You know, when Mama was okay, she was wonderful. I guess that was what made it so hard when she wasn't."

"It must be something that runs in our family. Mama and Aunt Dora; you and Sylvia. Sisters, one strong and one weak. How do you figure that, Rosalyn?"

"It's in the genes, has to be. I was lucky, Sylvia wasn't. She got dealt a bad hand. More hot water?"

"No, thank you." Selma shifted her weight in the chair and examined the large bruise on the back of her hand. "Getting old's the pits." She said.

"You want to watch TV?"

"I can watch TV in Memphis. I'd rather talk."

"Well, I'll take you into the den."

Rosalyn had converted her second bedroom into a sitting-room/office, which she called the den. The sofa opened up into a double bed, but Selma slept in the other twin bed in Rosalyn's room when she visited.

"Sylvia was such a sweet child, Rosalyn, so loving. I always had a special bond with her. Maybe it was because I was there from the beginning. But she was always sensitive. She took things so much to heart. Do you remember that time we went with our mothers down on Third Avenue?"

"Selma, we went almost every week."

"I'm thinking about the time when Sylvia and I snuck in the back of Friedman's Kosher Delicatessen. We had been to the farmers' market, and Mama and Dora had bought chickens for *Shabbos*. Then we had driven over to Third Avenue in Aunt Dora's car. You remember, that black Franklin with the honk that went oogah, oogah. Your mama loved that car. She was so proud of being able to drive, of having a car of her own. Anyway we drove over to Third to Friedman's Deli, so they could get the chicken's *shechted*."

"I hated that whole thing," Rosalyn said, turning up her nose. "I have a phobia about birds. It's the feathers and the flapping, I think. Remember how Aunt Minnie and Mama would go into that pen to pick out the plumpest chickens? I don't know how they could do that. Oh, I hated the smell! The chicken man would truss their legs and fold their wings, so they couldn't move, and put them in a wooden box. Mama would put that box in the car, on the seat between us. The chickens couldn't move, but I could feel their aliveness and one big eye would always be looking at us. I would hear their throaty chicken sounds, and even if it was a hot summer day, they would give me chills. I could never bring myself to eat chicken, even to this day. Did you know that, Selma?

When we'd get out of the car on Third, Mama would hand me a dime and say, 'Shoshanale, this is for lemonade. Don't you girls get into any trouble, and meet us back at Friedman's.' You and Sylvia and I would take off to the lemonade stand. Remember how good that lemonade tasted? Then we'd stop by Mayer's Bakery on the way back. Mrs. Mayer always gave us something delicious and never charged us."

"Sylvia liked Friedman's best," Selma added. "As soon as she would see it, she'd break away from my grip and race into the store."

"She liked those dill pickles Mr. Friedman gave us."

"Umm, yes. And the whole place smelled like fresh rye bread and horseradish mustard."

"Remember that glass case with all the corned beef and pickled tongue?"

"We haven't had a place like that in Nashville in years. You can't get kosher food anywhere. Maybe a few things in the grocery, but nothing you'd want."

"Those were good days."

"Good and bad."

"True."

"This one time, Sylvia pulled me through the curtained doorway that led to the back of Friedman's. We had never been back there, but Sylvia had watched James, the black helper, go in and out of that doorway with the beaded strings hanging from it and found it irresistible. For some reason you didn't go, Rosalyn. I knew we were overstepping our bounds, but Sylvia was insistent. We walked through that doorway into the storeroom. It was dark except for a single bare bulb that hung from the ceiling, but sunlight was pouring in the open back door. There was a fenced in backyard behind the store. We had no idea that we were going to see what we saw."

"Which was?"

"Standing behind a long wooden table was Mr. Goldberg, the *shochet*. Do you remember him? He had a long black beard, and his fingernails were always grimy. He had a dirty apron over his clothes and wore a beret. Remember when your papa would tell us those scary stories? He always made Mr. Goldberg the villain. And there we were, Sylvia and I, face to face with him!"

The doorbell rang. Rosalyn got up to answer it and returned with Lee Ann trailing behind. "Lee Ann's here, Selma. Sit down, honey, and I'll bring you some coffee."

"Hello, darling," said Selma. "Come sit beside me."

Lee Ann dropped down on the apricot sofa and tossed one of the needlepoint pillows aside.

"Whew, what a day! What have you guys been up to?"

"Just talking. About Sylvia, mainly."

"Oh, it's that time of year again, isn't it?"

"I was telling your mother about the time Sylvia and I snuck into the back of Friedman's Deli."

"You did what?"

"We snuck into the back of Friedman's."

Lee Ann snickered. "You just have to excuse me, Aunt Selma, but I can't imagine you sneaking in anywhere."

"I was young once, you know."

Rosalyn returned with the coffee. "Would you like some strawberry shortcake?"

"No thanks, Mom. Aunt Selma was just telling me about the time she and Aunt Sylvia snuck into Friedman's."

When Selma wasn't looking, Rosalyn mouthed to Lee Ann, "For the 100th time."

"So what happened, Aunt Selma?"

"Well, Mr. Goldberg, the shochet was standing behind a long table and as scary a character as you would ever want to meet. He couldn't see us because we were in the shadow of the wall, but we could see him. He picked up a long knife off the table, put the blade against a wheel and began working a treadle with his foot. Sparks began to fly as he sharpened the blade. He stopped, blew on the blade, then carefully ran his finger down the side. He laid the knife on the table and reached down and picked up one of our chickens from the chicken box.

"I hadn't noticed it before but there was a board propped up behind him, a board with pegs projecting from it. Mr. Goldberg laid that chicken's scrawny neck across the peg. He picked up the knife and in a flash had slit the chicken's neck. Blood spurted out and the chicken jerked violently. Mr. Goldberg held it by its feet and blood ran all over the ground. As he hung those trussed feet of the now-dead chicken over a peg, I felt Sylvia swoon beside me."

"She fainted?" asked Lee Ann.

"Oh yes, and of course we were discovered. Aunt Dora was livid.

It was a spectacle, and if there was one thing Dora hated, it was a spectacle."

"And what about Aunt Sylvia?"

"They put a damp cloth on her head, and she came around soon enough. She was just a little thing, but she was mortified and Aunt Dora fussed at her all the way home. You would think she would have blamed me. After all, I was much older and should have known better, but it was Sylvia she took it out on."

"Sylvia had that effect on her," Rosalyn interjected. "The least little thing Sylvia would do would set Mama off. She didn't like the way Sylvia looked, either. She was too gangly, too thin. Her feet were two big. She was too pale. Her hair was too straight. You name it!"

"She was always comparing the two of you and, of course, you were perfect and could do no wrong," added Selma.

"You guys are doing a lot of Grandma Dora bashing."

"Oh, honey, it's not that, exactly. We know full well that she was a sick woman. It just helps us come to grips with the situation. We have Sylvia on our minds tonight, and you cannot separate out Sylvia from Mama."

"Still, I..."

"There are just incidents that are so ingrained in our memories, Selma's and mine. Hurtful incidents. The worst to me was the clown suit."

"Oh, my God!" wailed Selma.

"What happened?"

"I guess Sylvia was about nine or ten. There was going to a pageant at the YMHA. Sylvia had gotten a part in it. She was so excited. It was the biggest thing that ever happened to her. That's all she talked about. She practiced her part over and over. She was to be one of the clowns, and Mama was making her costume. It was one of those clown costumes. You know, one side was red and one side white, with big pompoms down the front and a red and white

pointed hat with a pompom on top. It was Sunday morning and the
pageant was that afternoon.

Mama was out on the sun porch in front of her sewing machine,
working on the costume. Sylvia knew she wasn't to disturb Mama
while she was working, but she stuck her head through the door to
see how Mama was doing.

'Go away, Sylvia!'

'But Mama, I want to see!'

'Go away, Sylvia!'

Fifteen minutes later she cracked the door open and peeped in.

'Go away, Sylvia!'

'Are you almost finished, Mama?'

At that, Mama turned off the machine, ripped the clown suit out
and tore it down the middle."

"That's awful! What happened then?"

"It was like Mama had ripped the heart right out of her. Papa and
I figured out what had happened right away, and Papa rushed the
costume over to Aunt Minnie's. She patched it up the best she could
and Sylvia was in the pageant, but she barely went through the
motions. There was no joy in her, no life. That night we had to take
Mama back to the sanatorium and thought we might have to take
Sylvia, too."

"Could they really help Grandma Dora at the sanatorium, or
was it just a place to get her out of the way?"

"It would help for a while, it really would. Especially when she
had the shock treatments. Sylvia got treatments out there, too, once
or twice."

"I always knew that Grandma was fragile, but I never thought of
Aunt Sylvia that way. She was always there for me during that time
she lived with us. You know, during the war. We were very close.
She always made me feel good, special, like I wasn't just a little kid
in everybody's way, but somebody with ideas and feelings. There
was an aura about her that I loved, those stacks of movie magazines,

the drawer filled with those little bottles of fingernail polish with the painted nail on them, that pale green rocker with the cane bottom that was always getting punctured, the *Tabu* perfume and those wonderful hats she used to wear.

I still miss her, after all these years. What was she? Twenty-five, when she died. Lord, I have children older than that! I remember so well the day Aunt Sylvia died. You sent me a message at school, Mama. I was in the fifth grade at the time. The message said that Aunt Sylvia was sick in the hospital, and that I should go home with Judy Kahn after Hebrew School. You never sent me messages at school, so I knew that it was something serious.

In those days we went to Hebrew School three afternoons a week, Aunt Selma — I don't know what we did there, we sure didn't learn Hebrew. Anyway, I walked over to the synagogue that afternoon and got there a little bit early. I put my book satchel on a desk and walked out in the hall. No one was around, so I slipped into the sanctuary. It was dark, I remember, the only light coming in through the floor length windows on either side of the pulpit. The rays of that afternoon sun bathed the *bima* in a golden light. I still had the childish idea that God lived inside the ark. I was very much in awe of that place.

It was the first time I ever prayed. Really prayed. Naturally, I had said the *Shema* and other prayers, but this was the first time I had said a personal prayer, a prayer from the heart. I told God about Aunt Sylvia being sick in the hospital and asked Him to make her well.

I bumped into Cantor Fine as I came out, and he asked me what I was doing. I was embarrassed, but I told him the truth. I'll never forget the look on his face. It was pain and it puzzled me. What he knew, of course, and I didn't, was that Aunt Sylvia had already died. I didn't know until later, after I got to Judy Kahn's. We were playing Pick Up Sticks on her mother's tile bathroom floor when Mrs. Kahn came in and told me. You would have thought that I would have run off crying but I didn't; I just kept on playing and didn't even look up.

Later Grandma Pearl came for me, and I stayed at her house until after the funeral. Then you came, Mama, and took me over to see Papa Jake and Grandma Dora. They were sitting *Shiva*. The house was filled with people, everyone was talking and smoking, and all the mirrors had been covered with sheets. You told me that was so the Angel of Death wouldn't be reflected on anyone else in the family. It's funny how some things stick with you."

The phone rang and Rosalyn answered it. Lee Ann and Selma talked quietly until she was finished.

The Gay Street Jewish Synagogue — Conservative — 1902-1947

"I was just saying to Aunt Selma that I really couldn't remember exactly what Aunt Sylvia died from," said Lee Ann, as her mother hung up the phone.

Rosalyn's eyes met Selma's. "She died of a stomach disorder."

"But she hadn't been sick. I remember that distinctly. She hadn't been sick. What sort of stomach disorder was it?"

"If you don't mind," said Selma. "I'll go to bed now. I am suddenly very tired."

"I'll take you," responded Lee Ann, getting up.

"Never you mind, I can manage. You stay here and talk to your mother."

"Good night."

"Sleep well."

Rosalyn and Lee Ann watched Selma wheel herself out of the room.

"Can she really manage by herself?" asked Lee Ann.

"Oh, yes. She does fine. The chair is just for her heart condition, and it also takes the weight off her hip, but she's not a cripple. She can take care of her needs."

"What was that all about?"

"What?"

"Her hasty departure."

"I don't know what you mean."

"Oh, come on, Mom. Aunt Selma would never simply pull out of a conversation. She never wants to miss out on anything. She was deliberately leaving us alone. Why?"

Rosalyn pulled a half-finished sweater out of her knitting bag and began examining the stitches.

"You're stalling, Mama."

Rosalyn looked up. "There just was never any reason to tell you." Rosalyn stood up. "I'm going to get some more coffee, you want some?"

"I'll come with you," Lee Ann said, following her mother into the kitchen. She was always amazed at her mother's kitchen. Everything was in place and spotless. It had always been so, even when she and Lori Sue were kids. But the whole house was like that, neat and tidy. The colors were warm and inviting, the furnishings comfortable, but the environment Rosalyn created around herself was one of order, of completion. There were no loose ends with her. And yet, now, this woman who loved to share her life with everyone, had something she had never told her own daughter.

They sat down at the dinette table and Rosalyn began to talk. "It is very difficult when you have kept something locked up inside for so many years, when you didn't dare speak of it." She took a sip of the coffee.

"There were times when I really wanted to tell you. You were too young, of course, when it happened. But later, when you were older, I just never could get the words out. Once the funeral was over, I never spoke of it; not to my parents, nor George, nor even Selma. Selma and I talk around it. It's always there in the background. Selma was one of the few people outside the immediate family who knew...who knew the whole story."

Lee Ann could see the sadness etched on her mother's face. She looked uncharacteristically weary.

"Sylvia poisoned herself."

Lee Ann could feel the tears welling up. Aunt Sylvia, her sweet, loving Aunt Sylvia killed herself!

"My God, why, Mama?"

"You heard us talking. Sylvia had a difficult childhood, an unloving mother. I guess I was to blame, too. I was the older sister, the popular one, the one who always got good grades, who always got invited to parties. Everything seemed to affect her more deeply. It was like she had a heightened sensitivity. It didn't serve her well. She tried so hard. She tried hard in school; she tried hard to please Mama; she tried to be popular, but basically she was unhappy. And at times depressed. But never with you, Lee Ann. With you, she was totally comfortable. She loved you so much." Rosalyn dabbed at her cheek with her napkin.

"Then the thing happened that pushed her over."

Rosalyn looked down at the brown liquid in her cup, seemingly trying to look through it. Lee Ann sat very quietly and studied her mother. The white hair was tastefully coifed. Her skin, though wrinkled and softened, had a flawless quality. Even at seventy-five, she was a handsome woman. People noticed her...her careful dress and ready smile. At times, Lee Ann thought her frivolous, but now she wondered how well she really knew her.

"During the war, she lived with us. She was such a comfort to me, having been left with all that responsibility...running the business, taking care of two small children, having my husband far away and in danger. I don't know how I did it. But Sylvia was there, and that helped so much. She was working at Castner-Knotts Department Store at that time. You know, the old one downtown. During the war, there were lots of soldiers around, Jewish boys, mostly from up East. Stationed at Camp Campbell or Smyna Air Force Base. They'd come into Nashville on the weekends, and Sylvia dated a lot of them.

"Then the war was over and Daddy came home. The soldiers went back to their lives, and Sylvia went back to live with Grandma Dora and Papa Jake. In those days, a single woman didn't live alone. She still worked at Castners, but things were different. All the intensity, the flurry of activity during the war was gone. Who needed her now? It's no wonder she was depressed. Her friends were starting families, and she was still unmarried at twenty-four."

"With so much going on, our minds really weren't on Sylvia. Once or twice Grandma Dora mentioned that Sylvia was putting on weight. But she was always finding fault with Sylvia. It never entered our minds." Rosalyn stopped, took off her glasses and rubbed the sides of her nose.

"She was five months pregnant before we knew."

"Pregnant? Aunt Sylvia was pregnant? How could that be? Why wouldn't I have known?!"

Rosalyn went on. "We all panicked! It was too late to do anything about it. Grandma Dora, Papa Jake — we didn't know what to do. Things like that just didn't happen in nice Jewish families. Not in those days, not in Nashville. Can you imagine if it had gotten out? People's tongues wagging. Us not being able to hold our heads up. We couldn't let that happen! And Sylvia wouldn't cooperate. She wouldn't tell us who the father was. In fact, she hardly said anything. Grandma Dora went to pieces, and Papa Jake wasn't much help either. It all fell on me."

Lee Ann's head was reeling. "I don't believe this. Aunt Sylvia pregnant. You didn't know who the father was?"

"She wouldn't tell. Never told anyone. She had gone out with different guys. Nobody special. She refused to say. And we never figured it out."

"My God! What did you do?"

"We were going crazy. And then I thought about Aunt Goldie in Seattle. God bless her. Uncle Herman had died not long before. So we sent Sylvia to her. Everyone thought she went because Aunt Goldie was lonely. That's what we said. After the baby was born she came home."

Lee Ann waited for her mother to continue. Rosalyn just sat there staring into space.

Lee Ann broke the silence. "And the baby?"

"Oh, yes, she had it in Seattle, and afterwards she came home. It was a girl. Sylvia never saw it. It was given for adoption right away."

"And that's it?"

"Isn't that enough?"

"Oh, my God, Mama. This is too cruel to believe!"

"What's cruel? It's the only thing we could have done. The only way. Don't think we didn't agonize over it. She couldn't stay in Nashville. It would have ruined her. The family couldn't have held its head up. She couldn't come back with a baby. There was no such thing as single mothers in those days. It wasn't 1991, it was 1946! Nobody got divorced. There were no unwed mothers. Widows with children, that was it. No single mother adoptions, no artificial inseminations. Nice Jewish girls did not get pregnant, have babies. Poor white trash, they were the only ones."

"Excuse me, Mama, I have to go to the bathroom. I'll be right back."

Lee Ann hurried down the hallway to the bathroom. She felt the need to return quickly, not to leave her mother alone too long. Her mind was racing, thoughts were tumbling, and below it all was rage.

How could they do that? she thought. It's no wonder she killed herself. My God, she must have been devastated! The shame, the embarrassment! But what is that compared to giving up the baby you have given life to, have carried in your body for nine months. And Mama, why didn't she stand up for her, help her. Why didn't I know any of this? I was nine and I was smart. Surely I would have picked up on some of the tension at least. Why was I so oblivious? I do remember her coming back from Seattle. I remember we took a walk, just the two of us, around the neighborhood. I asked her if she wasn't glad to be back home, to see all of us. I thought she would say, "Oh, yes," but she hadn't. She just smiled a sad smile, and I knew she wasn't. But that was all, that was the only thing, and I don't even know why I remember that. Why hadn't Mama said anything before now? Maybe she was afraid to tell me, afraid I'd judge her. Well, maybe she was right.

Lee Ann flushed the toilet, washed and dried her hands, and started back down the hall. Be careful, Lee Ann, she told herself. Don't blurt out anything, don't say anything you'll regret later.

Rosalyn was at the sink, rinsing out the coffee cups. When she turned around, Lee Ann could see she had been crying.

"She didn't talk about it when she came back. Never said a word. And I didn't bring it up. We just locked it away somewhere. I honestly didn't know how deeply scarred she was. I thought she just wanted to put it behind her. I should have known. I already had two children. Why did I think she wouldn't care? Then coming back home to live again with Mama and Papa. I didn't think, that's what. I just didn't think. And then I got the call from Papa Jake...Sylvia was in the hospital...poison.

She was still alive and fully conscious when I got there. We were able to talk. She hadn't regretted taking the poison. She said life had no meaning for her...that she was prepared to die. She said she welcomed it. I sat there for an hour and watched her die."

The phone rang. Rosalyn reached over and answered it. "Hello, David darling, how are you? Yes, she's still here. Just a minute."

She handed the phone to Lee Ann. "It's your hubby."

"Hi, honey. I'm here. We got talking and I lost track of the time. I'll be home in a few minutes. See you."

"I didn't realize how late it was, Mama. Guess I'd better head out." Lee Ann picked up her bag and stood up. "Mama, I don't really know what to say. I am overwhelmed by all of this. Why did you never tell me?"

"Lee Ann, you were just nine years old. Besides it was unspeakable."

"But Mama, I'm fifty-three. You surely could have told me before now."

"We couldn't tell anyone. So many lives would have been ruined. You mustn't tell anyone, Lee Ann."

"What difference would it make? Aunt Sylvia's life was ruined anyway. Grandma Dora and Papa Jake have been dead for years. There's hardly anybody left who even knew them."

"You're right. I know you're right, but I could never let go."

"Well, I'm glad you finally did." Lee Ann reached over and put her arm around her mother. "It's a terrible burden to carry alone."

Rosalyn sighed. "You better go, David will worry."

"You going to be all right?"

"Don't worry about me. I'm a tough old bird."

Rosalyn saw Lee Ann to the door and kissed her goodbye. "Call me tomorrow."

She walked back into the den and switched on the *Late Show*, keeping the volume low so as not to wake Selma. She would put off going to bed as long as she could. That flutter had started in her chest, the foreboding that had become all too familiar. She would have the dream again tonight, the nightmare. She was sure of it. There would be a knock at the front door and she would go and answer it. A tall thin woman would be standing there. Someone she didn't know. The woman would speak to her. "I'm looking for Sylvia Silverstein," she would say. "I believe she's my mother."

BOBBY RAY
LOVES NADINE

❦ 1991 ❧

"Now you take care Miz Becky and have a real good time,"
William said grinning broadly, his head moving side to side
ever so slightly, the involuntary movement of advanced age. He
produced a small square package from his jacket pocket. "This
here's for Miss Jennifer from ole Will," he said, pressing it onto her
hand. "I sho kin't believe she's gettin married." Rebecca Greenberg
nodded, then reached for the hand-rail and climbed up on the
Greyhound bus. As she made her way down the aisle, a familiar face
greeted her. "How you doing, Miz Becky? We sure do miss
you...and Mr. Solly." She smiled, clasped the hand and continued
down the aisle. She was looking for a window seat. Finding one, she
quickly squeezed past the young man sitting on the aisle, not even
waiting for him to stand up. She opened her large purse and put
William's gift inside. Through the window she could see him
standing there under the Glasgow, Kentucky sign, watching as the
bus pulled out, seeing her off...a slightly stooped gray-haired black
man wearing a navy blue suit that had once belonged to her
husband.

Attentive, she thought, so attentive...since Solly died. "Mr.
Solly wouldn't want me to let you go traipsing around at night by
yourself," he'd say, or "It's Mr. Carl's birthday today, did you
remember?" And every two thousand miles like clockwork, "I ran
your car down to Smythe's. It was time for an oil change." The bus

lurched, then moved forward with a surge of fuel-scented power, and she lost sight of him. What would I do without William, she thought.

From the very beginning... William was there... fifty years ago next month... when Solly and I came to Glasgow. Just the three of us then... Solly, William and I. William was the stockboy and handyman. I paid the bills, kept the books, stood at the cash register on Saturdays. My legs ache just thinking about all those hours I stood there, ringing up the sales, greeting the customers by name, passing the time of day. And Solly, he was everywhere, doing everything. That Solly could sell! Sometimes I wondered if they bought things because they needed them or because they just wanted Solly to talk to them, to be near them. I know the women did. The women adored him. I watched him like a hawk... but he never seemed to notice those women. Solly loved me. He loved me. God, we were young. What *chutzpah* we had... opening that store. Solly made the sign himself — Solomon's — Glasgow's Largest and Fastest Growing Department Store. Largest... it wasn't even as big as the entrance is now.

Becky took a deep breath and let out a long, low sigh that caught the attention of the passenger beside her. She felt his glance but kept her eyes on her hands folded atop her purse. She could see his worn blue jeans and washed white sneakers out of the corner of her eye. A small silver transistor radio was balanced on one knee. A farmer, she guessed, looking at his hands. She raised her head slightly and took a quick look at his face. Clean-shaven, sunburned, hair slicked back. Yeah, a farmer. Clean... scrubbed, Becky thought, smells good. Old Spice.

It struck Becky funny, his carrying a radio, no earphones stuck in his ears. It's kind of healthy really, she thought. Folks with earphones always seem so isolated... sitting there... heads bobbing up and down, bleary eyed. "I'm so tired and all alone," drawled the vocalist. There was something comforting about the radio. She offered the young man a smile but he missed it.

She turned toward the window. A child had made a smeary finger painting across it. "They just don't keep things up any more," she thought and reached into her purse for a tissue. She spit on the tissue and worked at the smudge.

Carl had wanted her to drive the car to Nashville. "Why don't you drive to the wedding, Mama? Let William drive you, and he can take the bus back. That way you'll have a car while you're here."

"The bus is fine," Becky told him.

"But Mama, you're a well-to-do woman, and you've got that brand new Lincoln. Why not be comfortable?"

"Don't aggravate me, Carl. I'm taking the bus."

Maybe I would have taken the car if Carl hadn't pushed so hard, she thought. Stubborn. I'm stubborn...always was. Right Solly? You used to call me the stubbornest white woman in Kentucky. Besides, I like the bus. You get to see people, see the countryside.

The Old Nashville Bus Station

She studied the window. The smudge was gone. For a minute she caught her sunlit reflection in the window...the two large orbs of her glasses and the outline of her face. She reached up and stroked the loose skin of her neck. If I could only wipe this away, she thought, I'd still be damned good-looking. She had played with the idea of a face lift years ago...but all that pain. And for what?

She leaned her head against the seat back, closed her eyes and let the country music lull her. Carl said Harry Roth asked about her all the time. "I think he's got his eye on you, Mama."

Harry Roth, Solly. You remember him? He went to high school with us in Nashville. Took me to the Purim Ball that time. Pissed you off. Me and Harry Roth...you wouldn't like that, would you, Solly? He called me last spring. Wanted me to come to Nashville...go to the symphony. I said it was too soon...too soon. He's an accountant, for God's sake. You know how laced up they are. I'm not going to get married again, Solly. Who needs that aggravation? Taking care of some old man. It wouldn't be like us, Solly. Not like you.

Sometimes...last night. I was sitting on the couch watching a real good story on TV. I was sitting there watching and crying. You know how I love to cry. You, too, Solly. We'd be sitting there watching one of those programs we liked so much. The tears would be running down my face and I'd look over. Your cheeks would be all wet. You'd look at me...give me that little smile...that private smile...and scoot over beside me...put your arms around me. I'd kiss that soft spot on your neck and play with the hairs on your chest. Becky's chin quivered. I miss that, Solly. It's no fun to cry anymore.

Becky opened her eyes and turned toward the window. The trees are beginning to turn early this year, she thought. Going to be a cold winter. That red one. It's a beauty. My God, look at that! In the distance a bluff jutted out from among the trees. On its weather-smoothed surface in bold black letters was written *BOBBY RAY*

LOVES NADINE. How did he do that? Get up there and do that. Must have planned it. Brought the paint and the brush. Was Nadine watching?

Sure she was. Watching and shrieking, "Bobby Ray, come down. Bobby Ray, you're crazy. You're gonna be killed. Come down from there." Yeah, Nadine was there all right, watching and protesting and loving every minute of it. When Bobby Ray did come down, they'd run to a grassy spot, pull their clothes off and make love right there. Becky chuckled. She could picture Nadine's mama, her hair up in curlers, holding Nadine's little pink bikini panties and saying, "Nadine, are these grass stains on your panties? How did you get grass stains on your panties?"

Bobby Ray was showing off. Right, Solly? You knew all about showing off. You did stuff like that. Crazy things. I loved it, too. You were so gorgeous.

"Five hundred miles from home," sang the man on the radio. I don't like going to Nashville so much anymore, Solly. Can't see much from the Interstate anyway. Not like the old days. Those country roads. Remember the Sundays...how we'd get in that old tan and maroon Chevrolet and drive down to Nashville...before we had Carl and Gloria. We'd take a picnic lunch. We kept kosher then. We'd stop and eat in that cute little park in Russellville. We'd stop in all the towns...walk around the squares...look in the store windows...check out the competition...see what they sold...how much they charged. Remember the people, Solly? The Kaplans in Bowling Green, the Simons in Russellville? Sometimes they would go with us. We'd dance until midnight at that nightclub...the one on Nine Mile Hill. What a dancer you were, Solly.

Becky looked down at the legs beside her. They didn't wear jeans back in our day, Solly. You would have been a knockout — those tight jeans curving around yours legs — around that tush. Levis used to be work clothes. Right, Solly? Overalls. We sold the living pee out of Levi overalls. Then somebody got the bright idea to make them sexy. Made piles of money, too, I bet.

We had a good time back in those days, didn't we, Solly? Remember Izzy Stein? God, was he funny. Remember the time I laughed so hard I wet my pants. I was pregnant with Gloria. Becky sighed. Kids don't have fun like we did. Not today. Jennifer and Randy. They just don't know how. It's not the same.

Carl wants me to move to Nashville, Solly. "Mama," he says, "Sell the house. It's too much for you to worry with. Come to Nashville. They've got these real nice high-rise condominiums, with doormen to carry your groceries and security systems. Lots of Jewish ladies live there. You wouldn't be lonely and we could look after you. You could go to synagogue. Join the Sisterhood. And the doctors. We have the best doctors and the finest hospitals in the South."

Oh, Carl, to be so smart, you can be so dumb. Don't worry, Solly, I'm not moving to Nashville. All those fancy Jewish women with their puffed up hair and jewelry. Harry Roth...those old men sniffing around me. Not for me, Solly. I'm country. And Carl's fancy friends, the Marlowes and the Alexanders. What do I have in common with them? I'd be an embarrassment. Carl and Emily. They'd get tired of me pretty quick. No, I'm staying in Glasgow!

Carl would meet her at the bus station, she supposed. He'd come himself...so dutiful, that Carl...in his tailored suits and handmade shirts. Jennifer's getting married, Solly. Our little Jennifer...all grown up. What a doll! And pretty! Like Gloria was. Why is it, Solly, why is it that I get along so well with Jennifer and I never hit it off with her daddy? And Gloria! Oh, Gloria. Becky shook her head. We didn't do right by Gloria, Solly.

Becky fumbled around in her purse and pulled out a small album...blue...with *Grandma's Bragging Book* written across the front. She flipped through until she found the faded photograph. So pretty, she was so pretty. Everybody that came in the store said,

"Miz Becky, that Gloria's the prettiest girl in Glasgow." Well, she's not pretty now. A miserable life, miserable. You cut her off, Solly. That was wrong. Most of it was our fault. If we had raised her in Nashville, maybe things would have been different.

I'll never forget that day as long as I live. "Mama," she said on the telephone. "I'm in Bowling Green with Glenn. We left school at lunch time. We got married, Mama. Glenn and I got married." Glenn Procter, that *shaigetz!* "I love him, Mama." What did she know? Not even eighteen.

You turned your back on her, Solly. For you it was Carl, always Carl. Carl's education, Carl's future. I can hear you now. "Look at that boy…a Vanderbilt graduate…head of his class…my son. And me…the son of a greenhorn." Your son! What about me, Solly? And Gloria, what did she get? A no-good husband who couldn't hold a job…a shlemiel. And those children…gevalt!

Becky pulled a clean tissue from her purse and blew her nose. She sniffed a couple of times, then stuffed the tissue into the ashtray on the armrest. Her chin jutted forward, her lips pressed together, the lower lip protruding slightly. I helped her, Solly. What else could I do? She would call — "Mama, I need money for the doctor." "Mama, the children need clothes." "Mama, the heat doesn't work." I helped her. I stole from you, Solly. I stole money from the store. Covered it up. You never knew. Becky's face softened. She lifted her head slightly and looked up at the clouds. You didn't know, did you? You didn't know and let me get away with it? Never mind, she'll be all right now — now that I am a rich woman. I've made provisions.

A rich woman! I guess we have to give credit to Carl for that. "Dad," he said. "Listen, I know you don't trust the stock market, but this company I'm with…it's going big time…going public. We are opening restaurants all over the country. I want you to take your savings, invest it all." And you did, Solly. You took our retirement money, bought the stock, and we got rich. Then I sold the store to a big chain and I got richer.

She felt the boy beside her move. He reached down between his legs and picked up his pack.

"You going to Nashville, son?" she asked.

"No, Ma'am, I'm stopping in Clarksville."

"You got kinfolks there."

The red of his sunburned face deepened. "No, Ma'am, going to see my girl."

Bobby Ray, Becky thought. Bobby Ray... going to see Nadine.

He reached into the pack and pulled out an orange and a paper napkin. Becky watched his broad fingers, as he tucked the transistor into his jacket pocket, then spread the napkin over his knees and began to peel the orange. She looked at the blond hairs that grew below his knuckles and wondered what it would feel like... to touch his hand. She felt a wave of heat pass through her and reached for a handle to open the window.

"Them things don't open up no more, Ma'am. Air-conditioning and all. You like a piece of orange?"

Becky waved her hand. "No, no thanks."

She turned back toward the window. My God, I'm lusting after a boy Randy's age... a farmer... on the bus! Becky leaned back and took a couple of deep breaths, expelling them slowly. She raised and rotated her shoulders. Her back had begun to ache and she suddenly felt tired. The bus seat made contact with her body in all the wrong places.

Maybe I should have taken the car, she thought. "You're a rich woman, Mama," Carl had said. A rich woman. I don't know what to do with all that money, Solly. I'm seventy-five years old. What do I need with all that money? I have taken care of the children. What would you do with it? Even when we didn't have money, you'd give it away. Anybody who came in the store. You'd reach in your pocket. Didn't matter who they were, what it was for. Remember the *schnorrers*, Solly? In their shabby black coats and beards...they looked so foreign, so out of place in Glasgow. They collected for everything — yeshivas, refugees, Israel.

How come we never went to Israel, Solly? Israel was right up your alley. Those tough people...starting out with nothing...the cards stacked against them. They were your kind of people. I think I'm going to go, Solly...go to Israel by myself. Maybe I'll go over there and start something. Maybe I'll take the money and build a school — the Solomon and Rebecca Greenberg School for...for what?...for something. I'll find something. What do you think, Solly? Me going to Israel.

Becky, wrapped in her own thoughts, hadn't realized the bus had come to a stop. Only the jostling in the seat behind her brought the awareness. Russellville. She craned her neck looking for the little park, but all she saw was a car wash...and a priest coming out of a church.

The *schnorrers* don't come to Glasgow any more, Solly. Not since I sold the store. Remember how you'd take them back to your little office and give them a shot of whiskey. You loved that, Solly, that Jewish contact. You always wanted to build a little synagogue, a *shul* in Glasgow. Where the Jews from all around could come on the holidays, make a *minyan* when there was a death. I could do that now. I could build a *shul*. Only...the people all died, their children moved away. Solly, I'm that last Jew in Glasgow.

Little chewing sounds...orange punctured by teeth. Beside her on the boy's napkin lay fat curls of orange peel. A few wedges remained. Driving to Florida...me and Poppa...a bag of oranges...peeling oranges...the juice running down my dry throat...down my fingers...so fresh, so sweet.

"You know, Bobby Ray," Becky said, "I think I will take a piece of orange."

Glossary of Yiddish Words

Alav hashalom . . . Peace be on him

Aleha hashalom . . . Peace be on her

Bima . . . . Pulpit

Bubbie . . . . Grandmother

Bubeleh . . . . A term of endearment

Chevrusah . . . . . Study partner

Chutzpah . . . . . . Nerve

Chutzpedihk . . . . Audacious

Gefilte fish . . . . . Chopped fish balls or patties

Gevalt . . . . A cry of dismay

Goyim . . . . Non-Jewish people

Hamish . . . . Homey

Kishke . . . . Stuffed derma

Meshugaas . . . . . Craziness

Minyan . . . . A quorum for prayer ???????

Mishpacha . . . . . Family

Pitsele . . . . Small one

Purim . . . . Jewish holiday, 14 of Adar

Reb . . . . Mr.; Rabbi

Rugelah . . . . . . Rolled-dough pastry filled with nuts and raisins

Schnorrers . . . . . Beggers; seekers of charity

Schochet . . . . . . Ritual slaughterer

Sha die kindr . . . . Quiet, the children

Shabbos. . . . . . . Sabbath

Shaigetz . . . . . . Non Jewish man

Shana Tova . . . . . Happy New Year

Shechita . . . . . . Ritual slaughter

Shechted . . . . . . Slaghtered

Sheina Meidl . . . . Pretty girl

Shema . . . . Hebrew prayer

Shiksa . . . . Non Jewish woman

Shiva . . . . Seven-day mourning period

Shlemiel . . . . . . Bungler

Shul . . . . Synagogue

Shvartzers . . . . . Blacks

Tata . . . . Father

Treif . . . . Non kosher

Tush . . . . Bathroom

Yeshiva . . . . . . Academy of Jewish learning

Yiches. . . . . Lineage

Yiddishkeit . . . . . Jewish custom

YMHA . . . . Young Men's Hebrew Association

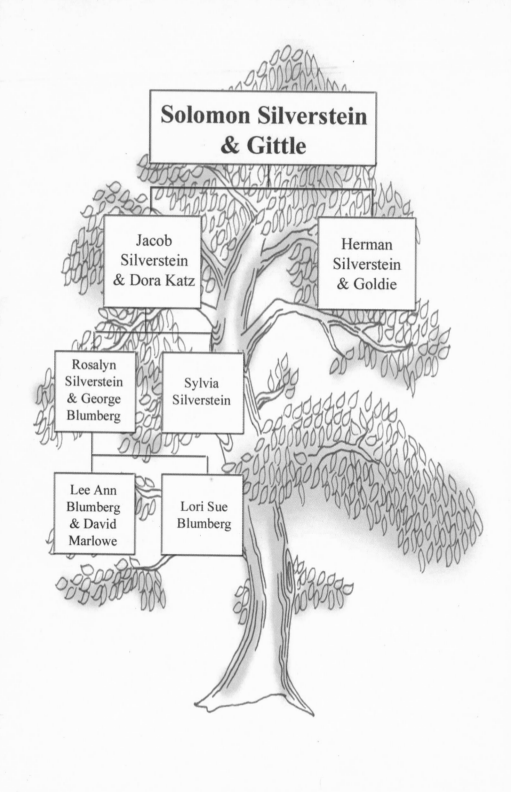